Farewell to the Glory Boys

A Battle of Arras Novel

Melvyn Fickling

By the writer of:

Bluebirds – *A Battle of Britain Novel*
Blackbirds – *A London Blitz Novel*
Falcons – *A Siege of Malta Novel*

Cover photo © David Stoddart
www.warbirdsphotographer.co.uk

Author Portrait by Moff Moffat

www.melvynfickling.com

Dedicated to Brian George Fickling (1931 - 2014)

For the sun may shine on the meadow lands

And the dog rose bloom in the lanes,

But I've only weeds in my garden, lad,

Wild weeds that are rank with the rains.

A verse from 'Easter' by

Geoffrey Anketell Studdert Kennedy

PART 1

SPLIT

Chapter 1

Thursday, 15 March 1917 – South of Arras

The approaching shapes grew larger in the eastern sky ratcheting the apprehension that tightened across Benn's shoulders. The shapes resolved into biplanes, their gaudy paintwork gleaming with dulled intensity in the insipid sunlight. He breathed a sigh of some relief to see the enemy flew at a considerably lower altitude, although they were climbing hard to close the gap. Benn looked left to where two other drab green Sopwith Pups bobbed in the bitterly cold wind, straining to interpret his flight commander's possible reaction to the developing situation.

Benn's attention switched back to the German formation as their labouring machines passed two hundred feet beneath his wings. With a lurch of hollow dread, he recognised the serrated trailing edge and elliptical tail-plane of the Albatros. The hunting pack of six German scouts curved into a lazy climbing bank, corralling the British machines as they steadily clawed away their disadvantage, the pilots' faces upturned to catch their quarry's first move.

Benn looked back to his leader's aircraft. 'We're outnumbered,' he muttered under his breath. 'Let's just climb away and head home.'

The flight commander caught his eye across the void, waved his hand in a circular motion, like a monarch in a race-day carriage parade, and side-slipped into a dive.

'Damn!' Benn pulled his goggles down over his eyes, swallowed against the fluttering in the pit of his stomach and hauled his Pup over onto its port wing to follow his two companions into the stoop. The Albatri flattened their climb and split into a wide fan, each jinking left and right, inviting the British scouts to engage against the stacked odds.

Benn chose a target, registering with disconnected clarity the lavender and mustard colouring on the topside and fuselage of his opponent. Air thudded across his wings and the struts flexed in protest as he hauled his Pup out of the dive behind his adversary and loosed off a burst of fire. He caught a flash of pale skin as the enemy pilot glanced back over his shoulder and spiralled his biplane into a dive. Benn matched the German's forward pitch, fixating on the other's white-painted tail section as the two planes dropped through the sky in fluttering tandem. He squeezed out burst after short burst, seeing, or imagining he saw, his bullets striking home through the wood and fabric of the enemy machine. He bunched his torso forward in response to the tingling premonition of danger that danced across the back of his neck, but he clenched his jaw fast against the desire to look back. Grappling to hold the Albatros in his sights he fired two more bursts – *'Damn, why wasn't the bastard dying?'* – then his resolve cracked.

Benn pulled hard on the control column and lurched out of the dive. The air around him hissed with streaking menace and staccato pops peppered the stretched canvas on his starboard wings with ragged black holes. An Albatros, this one mint-green and blue, flashed over his head and curved away into a shallow climb. Benn jinked violently, yawing left and right, searching the sky for his allies. There was no-one in sight except his attacker, banking to re-engage.

The Pup's engine mis-fired and coughed, rallied for a moment, then clonked to a standstill. *Out of fuel.*

Yowling with frustration, Benn shut off the throttle and threw the biplane into a tight spin, dropping vertically away from his tormentor. The slipstream whistled and slashed through the rigging as the contents of the landscape whirled around in a dun-coloured bowl edged by the spiralling horizon. Behind the wind-noise, the irritated stutter of the German's engine receded from his hearing as he fought against his dizziness to gauge his altitude. When the creeping fear of crashing outweighed the dread of flesh-ripping bullets, he kicked the biplane out of the spin and flattened into a shallow glide. Snaking in fat wallows to the left and right to avoid speculative small arms fire from the ground, he scanned the terrain around him with mounting urgency.

Long, ragged trenches scarred the landscape, but between them a tiny flat patch of earth miraculously beckoned from between the undulating shell-holes. Aiming at this unexpected sanctuary, Benn hauled back on the stick and dropped the Pup into a tail-down stall. The undercarriage thudded into the soft earth, throwing him hard against the instrument panel.

Heaving gulps of air into his winded lungs, Benn lolled out of the cockpit, bounced off the lower wing and splayed onto the hard ground. Rolling away from the plane, he lurched into a crouching lope towards the nearest shell-hole. Halting at the crater's edge he found it was half-full of murky water, the oily surface broken by a bloated grey-clad body half-submerged in its centre. He tottered towards another hole, ten yards distant. This one was new and still largely dry. He slid into the hollow over soil still scented with cordite from the explosion that had displaced it.

Benn arched his back to stretch away the cramps from his bruised torso and stared up at the sky. Aircraft moved silently against the cloud base. With their engine noise stolen by the wind, their drifting passage appeared ethereal and effortless. Benn squinted against the flat greyness, but the machines were too high to identify. He glanced around at the earth walls of his fragile sanctum and wished he could be up there with them, whoever they might be.

Only his own ragged wheezing disturbed the preternatural stillness. But something else permeated the rasping in his throat and he held his breath to better listen to the silence. The iron quietude hanging over the shell-hole grew steadily heavier, bearing down with a weight of expectation that suddenly broke into a fluid hiss of malice. The ground bucked and a shock wave hammered into Benn's refuge, ramming an agonising pulse of pressure into his ears. Another shell followed, then another. Benn instinctively opened his mouth wide against the waves of ear-cracking compression. The Germans had called down artillery onto his biplane, dispassionately despatching shells of splintering high explosive to seek him out, tear him to pieces, finish him off In futile defiance, he counted the explosions out loud, screaming the number into the flat quiescence through which the next detonation would drop.

Explosion followed explosion, punctuated by his hoarse and desperate cries from the shell-hole…

A roar like a crashing steam train and a plume of dank earth dropped fist-sized clods of clay to bounce and roll around him;

'Eight!'

Concussion jolted him further down the slope and lanced another stab of pain into his ear canals;

'Nine!'

The air split like tearing canvas, an errant blast, further away;

'Ten!'

Another rush of tortured air, another explosion still further away;

'Eleven.'

The ground lurched like a vomiting cat. Compression deafened him to the detonation just yards from his refuge.

'Twelve!'

Another followed it into the same spot. Concussion cuffed Benn's face against the soil.

'Thirteen!'

This last shout hung in the smoke-streaked air that thickened with a new, more sluggish silence as the frigid breeze swirled the acrid fumes of spent explosives down into his hole. Benn opened his eyes to stare at his knees bunched in desperate self-defence against his chest. He untangled his fingers where they were clamped across the top of his leather flying helmet and stretched his body out against the earth. Something sizzled nearby and he turned to find a hand-sized lump of hot, jagged metal jutting from the side of the crater, crackling the moisture from the clay just eighteen inches from his head. Benn squirmed away from the steaming fragment and pushed himself up to peep over the crater's edge. His Sopwith Pup sagged and smoked on the blasted earth. The shelling had reduced the aircraft to a bundle of mangled wreckage with its wings laying ragged and flat on the ground, like a rotting gull washed up on a beach.

The air next to Benn's face cracked with sudden transient violence and a bullet kicked dirt into his mouth. He cringed further down the slope, spitting begrimed saliva onto his chin. Another round gouged a second hollow slightly above his head. He jammed his chin down onto his chest, hugging his arms around his body to make himself as small as he could.

A third round cleaved the soil next to his face, followed in quick succession by two rifle-shots firing from a different direction.

'Get over here. Quickly!'

The sound of British accents galvanised Benn with a surge of wild hope. He took a deep, steadying breath and scrambled out of the crater. Glancing to his right he saw a motionless, grey-clad figure slumped over a rifle, horrifyingly close to his hiding place. To his left there were two dull-green domes sticking above a ridge of earth thirty yards away. British helmets, one nestled close along the sights of a rifle that aimed past him and beyond the crater.

'Run, man!'

Benn loped towards the helmets, stumbling over the rough ground, agonised by the exposure and cursing his thick, sheepskin flying suit. Gritting his teeth against the expected impact of bullets, he shuffled around a fresh, smoking shell-hole and dived between the two friendly helmets. He dropped into the trench, bounced off the fire-step and landed, sweating and breathless on the muddy duckboards at its base.

'Thank you,' he gasped.

The soldier with the rifle stepped down from the ledge, eyed Benn with detached disdain and walked away, vanishing around a dog-leg in the trench.

The other soldier squatted down on the fire-step.

'Best not to mention it.' He lit a cigarette and spat a stray shred of tobacco from the tip of his tongue.

Benn sat up: 'What do you mean?'

The man grimaced: 'That barrage you just brought down on us… one of the shells dropped straight into the trench' – he nodded towards the corner his companion had turned – 'a couple of our lads got badly torn up.'

'I had to land the bloody thing somewhere,' Benn said. 'I ran out of fuel. It's not my fault they decided to shell my kite.'

The soldier regarded him with a steady gaze over the glowing tip of his smoke.

'If running out of fuel isn't *your* fault, whose is it?'

Benn dropped his eyes and swallowed against the lump of embarrassment in his throat: 'I'm sorry.'

'Anyway, you'll not want to be hanging about here.' The soldier stepped down onto the duckboards. 'Follow this trench north for half-a-mile or so, you'll reach a communication trench that'll take you away from the line.'

The infantryman moved to follow his companion. Benn stood and half-raised his arms in spontaneous contrition to the man's retreating back. But no words came to his throat, so he turned and trudged in the other direction. The dreary grey sky dropped a swirl of fat, white snowflakes that danced in the frigid air and settled across his shoulders as he walked.

***

Vert Galant farm squatted in the centre of its fields, as it had for centuries past, bisected by a single-track road that meandered away to the north and the south. But now, the dilapidated farm buildings overlooked the meadows through shutter-less windows, abandoned by the family that had lived and thrived within their walls. Once a crucible of bucolic contentment, its sparse interior now served as scratch billets for flight commanders of the Royal Flying Corps.

Long empty of livestock, the grassy field across the road was filled instead with wooden huts scattered around canvas hangars where men bustled amongst the gawky frames of flying machines, oiling engines, tightening rigging and patching canvas. Vert Galant was now the home of Jackdaw Squadron.

Major Claypole strode past a hangar entrance, the strident stench of aircraft dope mixed with stale sweat tingled in his sinuses.

'When did you last see him?' Claypole said.

Captain Mumford walked beside the major, forced into an ungainly waddle by his flying suit. 'He dived after a Hun machine. They had the numbers, so I suspect another one followed him down. I didn't see him after that.'

'You were outnumbered' – Claypole cocked his head – 'and you still attacked?'

'We had good height advantage, sir. I thought it was worth a stab.'

Claypole looked at his watch: 'Well, I suppose there's still time for him to get back.'

'Actually, I'm not sure that there is.' Mumford swallowed nervously. 'You see, Benn never flies with a full tank.'

The major stopped and glared at the other man through narrowed eyes.

'I beg your pardon?'

'He has a morbid fear of fire, sir.'

'And you let him get away with this?'

Mumford looked down and said nothing.

A snowflake fluttered down between the men. Distracted, Claypole followed its progress to the grass where its edges blurred and melted, then he turned and strode away.

***

Benn sat at the western end of the communication trench, waiting for dusk to darken into night before making a move. A platoon of soldiers talked, smoked or dozed around him, also waiting for darkness to start their trek away from the lines. They had the easy demeanour of men at the end of a frontline stint, their minds at last diverted from constant danger. One open-faced young man looked at Benn's sheepskin garb with keen curiosity.

Benn caught his eye: 'I'm a pilot,' he explained. 'RFC.'

The lad's face split with a grin: 'Cor! What's it like?' He shook his head in wonder at the thought. 'Flying a plane! That must be a thing.'

Benn mirrored his smile.

'It's a bloody scary thing a lot of the time, but it's definitely quicker than walking.' He lifted a mud-caked flying boot off the ground and grimaced. 'Listen, I need to get back to my aerodrome, twelve miles north of Amiens. Do you know exactly where we are?'

'We're a spit south of Arras' – the boy nodded in the thickening gloom – 'so the first road you come to will take you west, directly towards Abbeville, if that helps.'

'Yes. I reckon that's a good enough start.'

'But mind yourself, the road runs parallel to the front-line and the German gunners generally work a nightshift.' The soldier smirked at his own grim joke.

'Come on, lads. Let's go.' A sergeant's voice dragged the platoon to their feet. 'Cigarettes out; no more smoking 'til we get where we're going.'

Pulling on their helmets, mumbling and yawning, the soldiers walked up the gentle slope and out of the trench entrance.

One cuffed the young man around the head as he passed: 'On your feet, Charlie, it's not a bloody social club.'

The boy moved to follow them.

'Good luck,' he said over his shoulder before he was swallowed up in the descending gloom and the retreating backs of his comrades.

Benn stood and held himself flat against the trench wall to let the rest of the soldiers stream past. As the last khaki-clad figure lurched by, he struck out on what he hoped was a westerly course. For a short distance he followed the soldiers' boot-prints in the thinly-settling snow. When these vanished into slush, the easterly breeze at his back kept him on track.

At intervals, single shells erupted into the night with lurid orange flashes. At first Benn crouched to the ground every time he heard one approach, but after half-an-hour he'd learnt to gauge a shell's likely proximity by the loudness of its approaching roar and shambled on untroubled by most of the rounds.

Beneath his feet the mud became clotted with rubble, getting denser and easier underfoot as he travelled further west. From this mix of earth and hard-core, a relatively undamaged road evolved from the ground. Shell-strikes, although still frequent, receded behind him as he made better progress on the solid surface.

On either side of the road, the slicing of spades through earth and the grunts of digging sappers murmured through the night. Benn squinted to make out small groups of silhouettes toiling in the distant darkness. Closer by the road he came upon a digging party excavating a circular hollow, shovelling the spoil into sandbags and building a defensive buttress around the eastern edge of the depression. One of the diggers watched him with sullen suspicion as he trudged past.

A mile further on, the snort and cough of equine exertion drifted towards him. He stepped off the road and waited. A pair of harnessed horses loomed out of the murk like some two-headed beast of ancient legend. The white stripes on their noses bobbed in unison and their breath condensed and curled around their chests as they laboured against their load. Alongside the beasts their driver plodded, his face lighting up in a faint orange patina with each draw he took on his stubby cigarette. The muffled clink of metal upon metal and the heavy thump of hooves against the road punctuated their progress. The horses dragged an artillery piece, its barrel swathed in mud-caked sacking, its carriage gliding in near-silence upon its heavily greased axles. As they passed, the snow redoubled, drawing a swirling white curtain into which the horses and their burden melted away, and from which the pair that followed them materialised.

Benn watched the second howitzer pass and the third appear after it. He turned his back to the slanting snow and shambled on along the rutted verge.

Friday, 16 March 1917 – Approaching Arras

The platoon straggled into a long line, snaking slowly through the darkness. The soldiers travelled in groups of two or three, each group separated from each other by a dozen yards or so. Shell-strikes ahead of them flashed the horizon into momentary relief, and an occasional flare, fired in speculative caution from the British front-line, cast a longer, sputtering light on their destination.

The British stronghold of Arras sat in a low depression in the land. The city was overlooked from the east by a concave arc of low hills, the northern arm of which formed Vimy Ridge. This high ground concealed the maze of deep trenches and tunnels that harboured the enemy forces that had occupied it for over two years. German artillery, entrenched on the eastern slopes, lobbed a desultory stream of shells into Arras, chipping away at the long-abandoned streets and houses, erasing its ancient Flemish legacy, wall by lintel, rafter by gable, and brick by broken brick.

Charlie found himself walking alongside one of a small handful of soldiers he'd bonded with while manning the trench they'd now left far behind.

'What do you reckon, Percy?' he asked.

'I reckon I'd kiss the Kaiser for a cigarette,' Percy replied. His eyes flitted around with every flash of light and guttering flare, intent on reading each glimpse of the landscape they afforded.

'I meant about what happens next, to us,' Charlie said.

'Considering *that* is what's left of Arras' – a flare blossomed in the distance, backlighting the jagged wreckage of the cityscape – 'and we're heading towards it, I suspect nothing very good will be happening for a good long while.'

'I had my heart rather set on a bath,' Charlie said.

'Oh!' Percy looked at his companion, his eyes crinkling at the imagined luxury. 'I'd kiss the Kaiser's *arse* for a bath.'

***

The snow swirling around the soldiers' heads sparkled with the breaking light of dawn as the platoon arrived at the southern outskirts of Arras. They bunched closer together as their sergeant led them down a rubble-strewn causeway into the city. Either side of them, the flamboyantly decorative facades of townhouses stood holed and desecrated. These broken carcasses of former opulence were topped with the exposed timbers of rakishly high-pitched roofs. The rafters clung to the surviving shingles that edged their gutters like the shredded hems of skirts. One building had succumbed fully to the depredations of incessant bombardment, leaving only a wrought iron spiral staircase that stood gaunt and askew amongst the dunes of plaster-dust and rubble. An ambulance drove past the small column of soldiers. Its driver, intent of avoiding rogue bricks in the road, showed no sign of noticing them.

The sergeant turned them left, heading west, away from the city centre. Some distance behind them, the whoosh of a descending shell terminated in the dull thud of its explosion and the brittle rush of cascading masonry. The men eyed the damaged walls that funnelled their progress and edged into the middle of the road.

As they progressed west, the buildings reduced in size and the signs of damage upon them lessened. They reached a small square that was lined with houses and the sergeant turned to address them.

'Gather round lads,' he called and waited for them to settle. 'We've been assigned as a labour unit to assist the Canadians in this sector.'

Groans and mutterings rippled through the assembly.

'Now, now' – the sergeant held up his hands to quell the mumblings – 'I know it's not what you were expecting, but something big is being planned and they need all the extra hands they can find. Whatever it is, it's better than the bloody trenches.'

Another explosion echoed around the shattered walls of the distant city centre, causing a ripple of movement as some men instinctively looked over their shoulders towards the sound.

'We're billeted in these houses,' the sergeant continued. 'They belong to people who might want to come back one day, so show some respect. Pal up and choose a gaffe. I'm off to organise some hot rations for us.'

Charlie and Percy looked around for their trench-mates. Jack, Trevor and Geordie gravitated towards them through the milling soldiers and the group moved towards one of the small houses. The windows were boarded up against blast and intrusion, but the door, caked in dust from the shell-pounded city showed signs of previous break-in. Charlie's hand hesitated over the handle.

'Hurry up Charlie,' Geordie chided. 'It's bloody snowing.'

Charlie pushed and the door opened, grating brick dust against the terracotta tiled floor. The others followed him in to a living room that still held all its furniture. A layer of dust covered everything, disturbed in places by the hands and boots of previous sheltering soldiers, and spent cigarettes and ration tins littered the floor. Otherwise, it was the home that it had been three short years ago.

'It looks like my nan's house,' Charlie said.

'I didn't know she entertained soldiers.' Percy dropped his backpack onto the floor and fumbled in his trench coat for his cigarettes. 'What's her address?'

Jack pulled back a curtain on the side wall and climbed the stairs it revealed.

'You leave my nan alone,' Charlie said. 'She's far too good for you.'

'Cor!' Jack's muffled voice travelled down the narrow staircase. 'There's beds up here. Mattresses and everything.'

'Well, well' – Percy exhaled a lungful of tobacco smoke – 'maybe this isn't so bad after all.'

Same day – Vert Galant

Thin slivers of dawn scratched at the sky outside. Despite a crackling fire glowing in the belly of the stove, the farmhouse was still cold enough for breath to condense around the breakfasting faces at the table. A smoky light leaked from paraffin lamps suspended on thin chains, assisting the nascent sunrise to illuminate the room.

Major Claypole chewed methodically, looking at the other men seated around the table with the demeanour of a mildly disturbed cat. Captain Mumford, still chagrined by Benn's disappearance, avoided catching his commander's eye. Captains Davenport, Hartley and Stiles munched on in enthusiastic oblivion.

Claypole pushed his plate away and drained his coffee mug.

'I understand we had some replacements arrive last night,' he said.

'Yes, sir' – Davenport nodded – 'half-a-dozen, I think.'

'Get them to fall in outside. I want to speak with them.'

Davenport laid down his cutlery and hurried out.

'I've arranged to run the new boys through some target practice,' Claypole announced. 'I thought it might be useful to discover what they're made of before things start getting dangerous.'

'Sounds like it could be fun,' Stiles said.

'Let's hope not.'

The clump of boots and a ripple of voices sounded outside. Claypole stood and retrieved his greatcoat from the coat-stand. Turning up the collar, he strode out of the door into the brightening day.

Outside the farmhouse, Davenport was marshalling six men into a ragged line. They shivered in the iron cold; faces wreathed in their condensed breath. Claypole stopped before the men and swept his gaze across them, drawing them to stiffer attention.

'Gentlemen,' he said, 'you've been sent to do an exacting and difficult job. But it's a job I've been doing on and off since this war started, so I like to think I'm rather good at it. I am Major Claypole, commander of Jackdaw

Squadron, and because I'm a friendly sort of chap, I'm going to give you a few hints and tips so you can use the King's aeroplanes to their best effect.'

As he spoke, he sauntered towards one end of the line and swaggered to a stop in front of the man standing there.

'Always stay in formation as long as possible. Formation flying is your sanctuary, your home and your family. Lone wolves are very soon dead wolves.' He looked into the man's eyes: 'What's your name?'

'Scarlett, sir.'

Claypole moved to the next man.

'Do not dive away from an engagement. The German is likely to be faster than you in the dive, but generally slower than you in the climb. You?'

'Hector, sir.'

On to the next man.

'Do not engage a superior force if it can be avoided. Rather, wait a few minutes to see if the situation alters in your favour.' He raised his eyebrows.

'Humphrey, sir.'

'Always look above and behind *before* you commence an attack. Odds are, if you have a German in your sights, you'll also have a German on your tail.'

'Morris, sir.'

'Do not fly low over the frontlines if you can possibly avoid it. You *will* get shot at by *both* sides.'

'Griffiths, sir.'

'And do not open fire too soon. Your bullets are obliged to obey gravity every bit as much as you are.'

'Cant.'

'I beg your pardon?'

'My name. It's Cant, sir.'

'I see.'

Claypole walked back to his position in front of the pilots.

'I know you've all been taught how to take off, fly in a straight line and land. Your arrival at my aerodrome suggests you've mastered that much. So, I want to find out how well you can shoot. The riggers have set up a ground target.' He gestured towards the far end of the field. 'Take off, one at a time, make three diving passes at the target and come in to land. Spotters will mark your accuracy. Dismiss.'

The six men hurried away to make ready, Claypole and Davenport retreated into the farmhouse.

In the far corner of the field, a grubby tarpaulin lay staked out over the grass, a large whitewashed cross marked its centre. Fifty yards away from the pinioned target, two spotters crouched in chilled misery atop a storage hut. One cradled a pair of binoculars, the other clutched a clipboard.

The first Pup coughed into life and taxied out onto the grass, an air mechanic at each wingtip, guiding it into position. The pilot waved and the men stepped back. With an ascending roar, the machine bounced across the grass, lifted into the breeze and soared away over the hedge into a climbing bank. The spotters on the roof watched it with despondent disinterest and huddled deeper into their greatcoats.

Inside the farmhouse, Claypole took the coffee-pot from the stove and poured the stewed, black liquid into his mug. The labouring engine noise outside thrummed the window with a sympathetic resonance and then the motor coughed and stuttered as the aircraft tipped into its first dive. Claypole gazed vacantly into space and waited. The spattering of the Pup's single machine gun broke his reverie and he looked up at the others seated at the table.

'I imagine things are going to get very busy quite soon, gentlemen. The campaigning season is just around the corner.'

'Surely not in this weather' – Hartley shook his head – 'if it's not pissing down, it's snowing. If it's not snowing, it's bloody freezing.'

'Campaign plans are made in front of a log fire with a glass of port to hand,' Claypole said. 'When those plans get to us, we'll have to carry them out regardless of the weather.'

'What's on the cards, sir?' Davenport's voice wobbled and he cleared his throat to hide his unease.

Claypole sighed.

'Oh, I don't know… Some kind of decisive offensive to drive the Germans out of France and end the war by Christmas. Something like that, I expect.'

'Didn't we try that last summer?' Mumford mumbled.

Another rattle of gunfire sounded across the field.

'If you can come up with a more original idea, I'm sure HQ will be keen to hear it.' Claypole placed his mug on the table. 'Come on, gentleman, let's go and see how the target practice is going.'

The five men crossed the road from the farmhouse, arriving in the field just as the second Pup opened up for its take-off run. They paused as it roared past them, then walked across to the hut bearing the spotters. As they arrived the first fighter swooped away from its third and final pass.

'Who was that?' Claypole shouted up to the spotters.

'Lieutenant Scarlett, sir.'

'How many hits?'

'None, sir.'

Claypole set his jaw against a twitch in his cheek.

'How is it possible…?' His question to no-one hung in the air as he scanned the sky for the second circling fighter. He found it clawing for altitude against the bone-grey clouds. It circled an ascending spiral twice more before levelling out and turning back towards the aerodrome. As it came over the field, the pilot rolled his aircraft into a dive, the engine note rising to a wail.

'He hasn't cut the engine,' Stiles gasped. 'What's he playing at?'

A long burst of machine gun fire rattled through the engine's roar and the tarpaulin target pitted and jumped with bullet strikes.

'Cut the engine and pull out,' Stiles murmured through gritted teeth.

The gun barked again, whacking another stream of bullets into the target. Then the engine-note changed, taking on a strained tone as the pilot pulled back hard on the stick.

With a sharp report, like a pistol shot, the wing-spar snapped. Both sets of wings slapped against the aircraft's flanks before tearing away in the slipstream, leaving the wingless fuselage to lance behind its squealing engine into the soft earth in the next field. The sudden silence filled with the hissing of ruptured fuel lines before the wreckage flowered into a ball of orange flame which settled into a crackling inferno, devouring broken wood and doped canvas.

The four flight commanders sprinted towards the wreckage. Claypole remained still, thrusting his hands into his greatcoat pockets.

'Who was that?' he called.

The shocked spotter took a moment to respond: 'Second Lieutenant Cant, sir.'

'Cant,' Claypole muttered to himself as he watched the broken wings fluttering to earth through the dense black smoke curling away from the crash site. 'Bloody poetic.'

Chapter 2

Saturday, 17 March 1917 – West of Arras

An insistent thump resonated through Benn's slumbering, like the throbbing waves of a bad hangover. For a moment the reverberation meshed into his dreaming, changing the course of already unfathomable events, then it overpowered his stupor with a tide of resurgent reality.

Benn opened his eyes and winced against the pain in his cricked neck. He lay in a shallow ditch next to the road under a dark sky that was beginning to accept the first dilution of dawn. He sat up into the renewed grip of the frozen air and blinked at the column of infantry marching their hobnail rhythm down the road and through the gloom.

The soldiers carried full packs topped with an entrenching tool, newly sharpened edges glinting in dull contrast to black-painted blades. Many hefted machine guns, trench-mortar tubes and tripods. Some men looked at him, eyes empty of concern, but most gazed mindlessly at the back of the man in front and all measured their pace by their own ragged breathing.

Benn dragged himself upright, champing against the leathery dryness of his tongue, and started along the ditch in the opposite direction to the flow of soldiery. The column snaked past, eventually exhausting its number with its advance. At its tail, a staff officer rode on the back of a chestnut horse. Benn climbed out of the ditch and waved the officer down. The horse stamped and pawed at the road, its nervous disquiet reflected in its rolling eyes.

'I'm heading for Vert Galant,' Benn called. 'It's close to Beauval. Am I on the right track?'

The officer braced against the reins and considered Benn's mud-caked sheepskin attire.

'RFC,' Benn offered. 'I had to force-land close to the frontline.'

The other man pointed back over his shoulder with his riding crop: 'You're a mile or two from Doullens. From there, the road heads south towards Beauval.'

'Thank you. Do you have any water?'

The officer's horse lurched forward at a jab of his spurs.

'Yes, thank you,' the man snapped as he cantered after the column.

Benn watched the officer's back recede as the sky ahead of his marching soldiers streaked with the strengthening light of the new day. He shifted his weight and grimaced at the warm '*pop*' of a blister bursting on his heel. A thin drizzle draped towards him on the breeze, reaching out to caress his face with icy fingers. He turned to the west and limped on.

***

One after the other, the four Sopwith Pups of Captain Hartley's flight bounced across the grass. They accelerated until their speed lent enough purchase to their juddering wings to haul them off the field and loft them into the air. Clawing up to a safe height and circling, they assembled in ragged formation, swung east and climbed towards the frontlines.

Claypole watched them vanish into the damp, grey sky, then strode across to the pilots' mess. He swung the door open and the murmur of conversations ground to a halt as men pulled themselves to their feet. Claypole gestured them down.

'Be seated, gentlemen.' He walked to the stove and held his gloved hands over its radiating heat. 'They're sending a truck for Cant later this morning. Does anyone want to accompany him to his burial?'

One of the other new arrivals shifted uneasily in his chair.

'No-one knew him, sir,' the man said. 'He arrived on a different transport to us. I think you're the only person who spoke to him.'

'I see.' Claypole gazed at his leather-covered fingers for a long moment as if pondering a point of order. 'Well, I need one of you to gather up his belongings and put them with the body.'

He started towards the door, but paused, distracted by something on the wall.

'What's this?' he asked.

More than a dozen scraps of brown paper were pinned to the rough planks, each cut to represent the silhouette of a man. Above the grouping someone had chalked the words *Jackdaw Squadron Contra Mundum*.

'The chief cook is a bit of an artist with a pair of scissors, sir.' Lieutenant Minton, a pilot in Davenport's flight, stood and joined the major by the wall. 'He used to do this on the front at Brighton for the day-trippers.'

'Am I on here?' Claypole searched from one paper pilot to the next.

'Yes, sir. At the top, naturally.'

'Ah, there I am.' Claypole beamed in recognition, then tilted his head towards Minton. 'And Cant? Is Cant there?'

Minton looked down at his feet: 'No, sir. There wasn't time.'

Claypole nodded slowly, looking again from paper face to paper face.

'I see,' he said. 'Too late now.' He turned and walked to the door. 'As you were, gentlemen.'

Outside, he pulled his collar up against the drifting drizzle and set off towards the farmhouse. Ahead, he saw a figure lurch slowly along the road and pass through the open gate onto the meadow. He stopped and waited. The man limped to a halt in front of him and saluted.

'Lieutenant Benn. I've come back, sir.'

'Ah, Benn.' Claypole nodded. 'You've come back from where, exactly?'

'I force-landed on the frontline near Arras, sir. I got down alright, but then they shelled my plane.'

'It was *my* plane, Benn. What took you so long to get back?'

'Yes, sir. Sorry, sir. I had to walk, sir. There's plenty of transport on the road, but it's all going in the other direction. May I have your permission to get back to the mess, sir? I think my boot is full of blood.'

Claypole nodded once. Benn saluted again and limped past him.

'One more thing, Benn.' Claypole spoke over his shoulder.

Benn paused and turned. 'Yes, sir?'

'If you ever take off with a half-full tank again, I will wait until you're in bed and personally set light to you as you sleep. Do you understand?'

'Yes, sir.'

Benn trailed across the grass and limped into the pilots' mess. Heads swivelled and conversations stopped.

'I've come back,' Benn said and limped to the nearest free chair. He sat, bending to pluck at his mud-caked boot laces.

'It looks like you've been on a hiking holiday, lad.' Lieutenant Minton poured a coffee from the pot on the stove. 'Did you have fun?' He handed Benn the steaming mug.

Benn sipped some of the black liquid and grimaced.

'I ran out of fuel,' he admitted.

'We did wonder.' Lieutenant Munnings stood warming his hands over the stove's hot plate. 'Captain Mumford had to tell Claypole about your half-a-tank malarkey, and he was not best pleased. You're lucky you're not on a charge.'

Benn stared down into his coffee.

'From what I've seen, I reckon the stockade would be the better place to spend the next couple of weeks,' Benn said.

The already quiet room solidified into stone silence and a dozen pallid faces turned towards Benn.

'They're digging new gun emplacements behind the lines,' he continued. 'There must be hundreds. Dozens of artillery pieces passed me on their way up in the dark. And companies of fresh infantry' – he looked from face to face – 'I even saw a staff officer on a horse.'

'Strewth,' Minton breathed.

'Yes.' Benn eyes dropped back to the contents of his mug. 'Something bloody big is brewing.'

'After last summer on the Somme?' Minton took a long draw from his pipe and blew a stream of smoke at the ceiling. 'Have they learned nothing from that bloody disaster?'

'You should hold the memories of last summer dear to your heart.' Benn spotted there were new arrivals, sitting at a table with hands of cards grasped in mittened fingers, and grimaced a sickly smile into their pale faces. 'Last summer the Germans didn't have the Albatros.'

Lieutenant Scarlett laid down his cards.

'What is it about this Albatros, then?' he asked. 'What makes it so special?'

Benn shook his head in mock despair: 'Didn't they tell you in flying school?'

'No, they did not.'

'Well, let me put you straight.' Benn's voice hardened. 'It's quicker than you in level flight and it's much faster than you in the dive, so you can't even run away from the bastards. The pilot is almost certainly better trained than you are, and even if he isn't, he's got two machine guns to your one. They very nearly did for me. I was lucky to get away.'

Benn pulled off his boot, wincing at the sight of his blackened sock.'

'Now, now, lad' – Minton's steady voice intervened – 'it is what it is. Let's not fret over what can't be changed.'

Benn glared from under his furrowed brow for a moment, then sagged back into his chair, 'They should be told,' he mumbled. 'They need to know what to expect.'

***

Captain Hartley levelled out at four thousand feet and squinted through the blur of the propeller to the lurid, earthen scars that marked the frontlines. Even at this height, the rusty banks of barbed wire were clearly visible, like skeletal tangles of autumnal bracken lining either side of the pock-marked valley of death that was no man's land. Along this desolate tract, an occasional eruption of mud marked the impact of an artillery shell, heaving the turgid, lifeless soil into new contortions.

He glanced to his right where Lieutenants Cobbit and Harkin flew in station. He looked left to where Lieutenant McGarry held formation, and a ripple of motion caught his eye. Way below McGarry's tail, a flight of five BE2s lumbered towards the front. As he watched, they banked onto a diagonal heading, aiming to bisect the lines. Muzzle flashes sparkled along the German trenches as riflemen and machine gunners opened fire, and larger blasts of smoke drifted from the muzzles of entrenched anti-aircraft guns. One of the bi-planes bucked with an impact and drifted out of formation. It rolled slowly onto its back and suddenly looped down into a spiralling dive to crumple against the mud in front of the British lines.

The rest of the planes lumbered on, traversing no man's land and banking slightly to follow the line of the German entrenchments. Desultory curves of tracer licked and swirled from the British observers' machine guns, like long, spidery legs momentarily connecting these angry flying insects to the ground. Small explosions burst across the ground in their wake as each pilot tossed grenades over the side.

A bright orange glow took root behind the engine of the leading plane, expanding and sweeping back with ravenous tongues of flame. The aircraft reared, stalled and dropped backwards into the barbed wire, buckling into the entanglement and splashing burning fuel through the impassive coils.

Hartley watched the three remaining machines break off their bombing run and veer towards the British lines, climbing hard to escape. Abruptly, the ground fire ceased and, a moment later, half-a-dozen sleek, coloured shapes slipped over from the east, sinuating like hungry fish above the retreating force.

'Damn it.' Hartley waved him arm wildly to signal his flight and pitched into a dive, pointing his Pup's nose directly towards the retreating bombers and their pursuers.

Two of the enemy scouts bobbed out of their dive and banked into a speculative climbing spiral. Ignoring them, Hartley chanced a long-range burst of fire in the direction of the other four, desperate to distract them from the BE2s. With a twist of his head, he saw that two of his flight had remained high, staying above the detached and circling Germans and so neutralising their threat. Only McGarry was with him, stuck to his port side.

Choosing the German at the edge of the pack, Hartley eased to starboard, squinting through the ring-and-bead sight and nudging his rudder to centralise the fighter wallowing towards him. The BE2s passed below, the chattering of the observers' defensive fire percolating through the engine racket. Hartley's Vickers gun topped off the cacophony and his tracers stabbed into his opponent's engine before the sleek, shark-like fuselage of the Albatros flashed by below him.

Hartley dragged hard into a half-loop, struts flexing under the pressure. Slowing at the apex of his manoeuvre, he scanned the scene. Another BE2 trailed thick smoke, flying incongruously straight and level, its fuselage and crew engulfed in flames, crossing the British line like a comet with paper wings. A different, thinner trail of blue smoke led his eyes to his recent opponent. Banking starboard, the damaged German machine dropped into a shallow dive in a dash to the east and safety.

Hartley's engine coughed in protest at his violent handling, then roared like a lion as he rolled into a dive to pursue the damaged Albatros, silently praying that Cobbit and Harkin would continue distracting its companions above him. Trading altitude for airspeed, he dropped in behind his limping enemy.

Too fast!

The wobbling German bi-plane loomed like disaster in his face. Hartley shut off his engine and pulled the trigger in one blind panic. Lines of tracer spanned the decreasing distance between the two craft, joining them like taught rigging wires. Splinters of wood spun from the struts around the enemy's cockpit, then a dozen puffs of dust burst from tiny holes that peppered the back of the German aviator's leather jacket. The man slumped over his controls and the Albatros nosed into a steep dive towards the ground.

Hartley restarted his engine and whipped into the steepest climb he dared to pull. The German wire slid by a few hundred feet beneath him. Two small holes popped into the canvas along his starboard wing. He twisted to check above and behind, but the hard sky lay empty. Another hole erupted in the port wing. Hartley looked down into the German trenches. At intervals a muzzle flash announced another rifle round seeking him out. He gritted his teeth and eased further back on the stick, maintaining an easterly course as he climbed out of danger. Two more bullets burst through the taut canvas, then he was beyond the lines, too high for accurate fire. He quartered the still empty sky for aircraft and levelled out.

Something in the east snagged his eye. A snake of massed soldiery traversed the snow-streaked earth. He flew on for a minute or so, squinting at the column until he could discern its direction of travel. Then he banked west and set his nose for home.

***

Hartley circled the field to approach into the wind. He smiled in relief to see the other three Pups from his flight already safely on the ground. His engine coughed and chuckled as he bounced along the rough grass and taxied to the edge of the field. Shutting off the fuel taps, he climbed out and shouted news of the damaged wings to approaching riggers. Satisfied they understood him, he strode across the field towards the farmhouse.

Major Claypole stood on the porch, watching the flow of activity rippling around the aerodrome. As Hartley approached, he swung the door open for him.

'Any business?' he asked, following Hartley into the building and closing the door against the chill.

'We came across a flight of BE2s bombing and strafing the German lines,' Hartley answered.

Claypole nodded silently.

'Two of them went down to ground fire, and then they ran into a circus of six Huns. I saw another one in flames before I got an Albatros for myself.' Hartley shrugged off his heavy flying jacket and sat at the table. 'What is the bloody point of sending these clowns on low-level bombing raids when we've got fields rammed full of artillery that can do a far better job?'

Claypole sucked his teeth: 'Well, it puts on a show for the foot-soldiers, I suppose.'

Hartley shook his head: 'It's bloody madness.'

Claypole shrugged: 'It's many months since I've seen something that wasn't.'

Hartley was silent for a moment beneath the hint of a frown.

'There's one more thing,' he said.

Claypole cocked his head.

'My scrap took me over the German lines. Before I turned back, I saw a long column of soldiers marching east.' Hartley raised his eyebrows. 'I think the Germans might be retreating.'

'Why on Earth would they be doing that?'

'Perhaps they're expecting a push?'

'It's springtime, Hartley. They'd be bloody foolish to expect anything else.'

Sunday, 18 March 1917 – Between Achicourt and Arras

Slatted duckboards stretched for fifty yards along one side of the road. Upon the boards, shells lay stacked, each horizontal layer alternating, up to a dozen high. The trucks delivering the shells had gouged ruts in the road. These had become runnels for the oily urine and manure of the horses that ferried the shells to the gun emplacements around the city. Charlie's mob stood in front of the ranked ordnance, stamping their feet against the morning's steely chill.

'I wonder' – condensed breath mixed with the cigarette smoke swathing Percy's face – 'what would happen if they managed to drop one into this little lot.'

'They'd have to post you missing in action, Percy,' Trevor said. 'On account of you being impossible to find.'

'Please don't,' Charlie said. 'I promised my mum I'd go back.'

'How old are you, Charlie?' Geordie asked.

'I told the recruiting sergeant I was eighteen,' Charlie said. 'So, that's what I am.'

'You shouldn't have left your mum in the first place,' Percy said. 'It's not right, lad. Not if you're underage.'

'Well, it's been a bit rougher than I expected.' Charlie looked around the faces of his companions. 'But now I'm here, I'm glad I came.'

'Here they come.' Jack pointed down the road. 'Customers.'

A pair of chestnut horses, harnessed to a simple four-wheeled carriage plodded towards them. The carriage bore two large metal containers, each centred over an axle. The team drew to a halt in front of the stacked shells. The team's driver cooed his appreciation to his beasts and walked back to unhitch the long side of the metal boxes. The sides hinged down to reveal metal sleeves, in four rows of ten, sized to snugly fit the ordnance. The driver leaned against the carriage wheel and lit a cigarette while the soldiers began handballing the shells off the stack and sliding them, fuse first, into the sleeves.

'What's the gossip?' Percy asked the driver.

'I hear tell that the Krauts are retreating, at least they are on the south side of the city,' the man answered.

'That's got to be a good thing,' Charlie said, carefully sliding a shell into place. 'Hasn't it?'

'Could be.' The driver screwed up his face in speculation. 'It rather depends on whereabouts they decide to stop.'

Chapter 3

Monday, 19 March 1917 – Vert Galant

Claypole stood with his back to the stove, lifting apart his greatcoat's vent to warm his buttocks as he watched Captain Stiles preparing for his patrol.

'I understand you're a bit older than me, Harry.'

'Yes, sir.'

Sitting at the table, Stiles opened a large pot of Vaseline, scooped two fingers into it and rubbed the slippery substance onto his face, contorting his features and tracking his progress in a shard of speckled mirror that he held in his other hand.

'I shall be twenty-six this year. God willing.'

'And there's a Mrs Stiles?' Claypole ventured.

'Indeed, there is' – Stiles surveyed his shiny visage with satisfaction and wiped the excess Vaseline from his fingers back into the jar – 'and I hope to see her for Easter. As you know, I've put in for the leave.'

'What the hell are you doing at the front in the first place?' Claypole asked. 'Surely, this is a game for bachelors.'

'Well, I was originally posted as a flying instructor' – Stiles unravelled a pair of thin white socks and pulled them onto his bare feet – 'but I found it too much of a strain.' He picked up a pair of thick hiking socks and examined the toes and heels for holes.

'I don't understand,' Claypole said. 'Flying instructor sounds like a dream posting.'

'I thought so too' – Stiles grunted with the effort of pulling the second pair of socks up and over his knees – 'but about half the intake were getting killed in accidents during their training. A fair few of them took their instructors with them.' He stood, pulled on his leather flying trousers and stamped his swaddled feet into a pair of fur-lined boots.

Claypole frowned: 'So, you volunteered for active service in order to feel safer?'

Stiles shrugged into his heavy leather flying jacket and fastened it.

'Not really, sir. I expected it would be touch-and-go in France' – he rummaged in his jacket pocket, pulled out a lady's silk stocking and stretched it carefully in his fingers - 'but I knew one thing: over here, I wouldn't have to face the dead boys' mothers.' He rolled the stocking down over his head, carefully positioning two pre-cut holes over his eyes.

'The mothers?'

Stiles produced a pair of white silk gloves from the other pocket and pulled them on with the care of a sommelier. He looked up, his face contorted like a friendly bank-robber.

'I had to greet them when they came to pick up the body. They'd always get into an awful state.'

He piled the excess stocking onto the top of his head and pulled on his fur-lined helmet.

'Imagine it. Their baby boy marches off with the noble intention of becoming a knight of the sky, and then he fucks himself up on his first solo landing. It's not what they expect, you see. Picking up a pine coffin from a shed in Hertfordshire wasn't part of their parenting plan.'

Stiles picked up his leather gauntlets, grimaced a farewell at his squadron commander through the sheer silk stretched across his face and clumped towards the door.

Outside the tufted grass stood stiff and white, crusted like coconut confectionery with crunchy ice. Stiles surveyed the sky as he crossed the road, squinting at the pendulous grey clouds waddling across the void, obscenely pregnant with rain, or worse, snow. From the sagging ridge of a barn behind him, a crow ducked its head to fix one eye on his back, its *caw* scratching at the frigid silence.

Stiles lumbered across the meadow, stepping over the frozen ruts, the toes of his boots splashed with wet streaks from the frosted grass. The muffled thud of stamping feet penetrated the fur pulled tight over his ears and he looked up to see the four other pilots of his flight, jiggling to stimulate circulation, their idle chat coalescing in a cloud of condensed breath that swathed their heads before fleeing on the light breeze. As he approached, the men fell silent and came to attention.

'As you were.'

Stiles recognised Lieutenants Platt and Potter. The other two were from the new intake. He squinted at them through the holes in his stocking: 'Remind me.'

'Second Lieutenant Morris, sir, and this is Second Lieutenant Griffiths.'

'How many hours in your log book, Morris?'

'Ten hours solo, sir.'

'On Pups?'

'Various types, sir. Flying to Vert Galant was my first time in a Pup.'

Stiles turned to Griffiths: 'And you?'

'Very much the same, sir. We trained together.'

Stiles forced what he hoped would escape the stricture of his stocking as a reassuring smile: 'Right, you need to listen to me.'

'Yes, sir!' Both men involuntarily jerked their backs a notch straighter.

'This is bloody important.' Stiles gestured at the line of aircraft awaiting them. 'The Sopwith Pup is a pretty little plane, but it's engine is under-powered. Consequently, it flies a tad slower than we would like. Because of this, it is vitally important that you hold formation whenever the enemy has the advantage. Once we're scattered, you have a far lower chance of getting home.'

He paused to let his message sink in.

'There are those who think the Pup is also under-armed. But I personally believe that if you're unable to kill a man with one machine gun, you should start looking for a different hobby.'

The pilots subdued laughter rolled another wave of condensed breath into the air around their heads.

Stiles pulled his cuff back to look at his watch: 'We take off in ten minutes. Platt and Potter form up to my port side, Morris and Griffiths on starboard. Any questions?

The four pilots shook their heads.

'Alright, gentlemen. Good luck.'

***

Stiles squinted into the buffeting wind, his eyes streaming from the pin-prick of icy air that seeped into his ill-fitting goggles. Running a patrol line parallel to the front on the British side, he'd completed several fruitless legs. On a whim, instead of doubling back to fly the same section again, he ploughed on towards the north. He glanced at the others in the formation, jabbing his gloved finger forwards to reassure them the change was intentional.

They ground on for almost two miles, then Stiles spotted puffs of smoke drifting through the air above the opposing lines. In amongst the bursting anti-aircraft shells were two dun-coloured BE2 biplanes, flying north, straight and level in tandem. Stiles waved him arm above his head to alert his flight and angled his nose towards the German lines to catch up with the other formation.

Three more shapes appeared above the labouring photo-planes and the puffs of smoke ceased. Still over half-a-mile distant, Stiles could do nothing but watch.

Two of the German aircraft dropped behind the leading British biplane, one close behind its port wing, the other splaying further out of its port side. Like a sheep rearing away from two dogs, the BE2 veered east, further into enemy territory. The second British biplane, confronted with its companion's hopeless situation, fled, banking west over no man's land, towards safety. Stiles started a shallow turn to converge with the fleeing plane, intending to protect its retreat. He glanced back at the other aircraft, jinking in front of the pursuing Albatri. A flash of movement snagged his eye and the third Albatros, red from nose to tail, sporting large black crosses in white-painted squares, dropped like a kestrel onto the corralled BE2's tail.

As the two herding Germans banked away, leaving their charge to the red predator, tracer blinked through the space between them. Stiles followed the tracer back to its source: a lone Pup, barrelling eastwards, firing long, speculative bursts that fell away below their target.

'Damn!' Stiles screwed his head around to see a single plane on his starboard quarter where there should be two. A flare of bright flame drew his eyes back to the action as the BE2 erupted into a fireball, folded its wings like a dying bird and swallow-dived earthwards, its red executioner banking sharply to watch it plummet.

The Pup also spiralled downwards in a desperate struggle to evade the two scouts it had attacked. But avoiding one took it into the gunsights of the other. Another brief burst of flame lit the winter sky and the Pup's spiral tightened into a dive.

Stiles looked away.

The British lines slid away behind them as he kept his formation of four scouts above and behind the retreating BE2 and its precious cargo of exposed photographic plates.

***

The four Pups circled the field before bouncing in to land one at a time. Groundcrew ran out to them, grabbing hold of wings and tails, and hauling the aircraft into a line at the edge of the field. Stiles climbed out and strode towards the farmhouse. Platt and Potter lingered for a moment to talk with riggers about adjustments to their aircraft before heading to the pilots' mess. Morris trailed behind them, leather helmet in hand and head drooping.

Stiles stamped up the steps and into the farmhouse. He tore his gauntlets from his hands and flung them across the room.

Claypole looked up from his paperwork.

'Is something the matter?' he drawled.

A flying helmet followed the gloves and Stiles sagged into a chair.

'I lost one of my flight.' He peeled the stocking from his head and wiped smut-flecked Vaseline from his cheeks with a grubby handkerchief.

Claypole watched the other's wispy hair rise and dance with static.

'These things happen. Who was it?'

'One of the new lads. It wasn't necessary; he bundled into a fight he didn't need to have.' Stiles looked up with a face creased by frustration. 'We stumbled on a recon flight, just before the Germans lit one of them up. There was no chance of helping them. He threw himself away for no good reason.' He settled his head in his hands. 'Honestly, if you ran a bus company this badly, you'd end up in court.'

'Which *one* of the new pilots?' Claypole persisted.

Stiles looked up and shook his head: 'God, I don't know. I can't remember his name.'

Claypole returned to his papers. 'Let me know when you do.'

***

The mess door swung open and the three pilots walked in. Platt and Potter, deep in conversation, shrugged off their jackets and walked to the stove. Morris followed them, closed the door and sat in the nearest available chair, eyes downcast.

'You saw it, didn't you?' Platt nudged his friend as he poured a coffee from the pot on the stovetop. 'The red Albatros. We've only got the bloody red Albatros in our sector. When *he* gets on your tail there's no hope of getting home.'

'Rubbish' – Potter rubbed the circulation back into his fingers – 'you can't make a scout more dangerous by painting it red. Anyway, I've heard rumours that the pilot is a young girl; a German Joan of Arc.'

'A woman?' Incredulity stretched Platt's voice. 'A *woman* flying an Albatros?'

'Why not?' Potter moved to sit down, pulling off his heavy flying boots. 'The other two did all the work. They delivered that BE2 to her on a plate, all she had to do was finish it off.' He nodded in satisfaction at his own logic. 'You don't need big muscles to pull a little trigger.'

'The *Daily Mail* says it's a member of the German nobility who flies that Albatros.' Minton's voice interrupted from across the room. 'They're calling him The Red Baron.'

'In any event, it's a bloody foolish thing to do' – Benn broke into the conversation – 'painting your kite red and getting a write-up in *The Mail*. Now every glory-seeking mother's son in the flying corps will be lusting after shooting down his arse.'

A speculative silence fell over the group, broken by Minton's quiet question: 'Didn't four of you go on that patrol?'

The words pulled a sob from the slumped figure in the chair by the door and all faces turned towards Morris.

He looked up with eyes brim-full of tears.

'Me and Griffiths went through flying school together.' Morris fought to control his wavering voice. 'He was the only friend I'd made since I left home.'

Benn stood and walked to the wall of silhouettes: 'Which one is him?'

Morris pointed, and Benn detached the face.

'Here,' – he handed the scrap of cut paper to Morris – 'a keepsake.'

The door swung open and Captain Hartley came in accompanied by a chill wave of snow-flecked air. The men all jumped to their feet.

'At ease, Jackdaw.' Hartley cast his eyes dispassionately about the room. 'My flight, get yourselves ready. HQ need another reconnaissance escort. We take off in ten minutes.'

Hartley wheeled out of the mess and four pilots hurried to the lockers to assemble their kit.

Tuesday, 20 March 1917 – Western outskirts of Arras

Percy hefted his spade and surveyed the meadow's scrubby grass. A block of nine rectangles were marked out with string pulled taut around wooden pegs. Each one was ten yards long and a little over two yards wide. A four-foot margin separated each from the other.

'Latrines?' Charlie speculated.

'Maybe, lad,' Percy said. 'But somehow I doubt it.' He set the blade of his entrenching tool flush against the string, set his boot on its shoulder and pushed it into the moist earth.

The platoon spread out, half-a-dozen soldiers to each rectangle. The sergeant, satisfied that his men would be occupied for several hours sidled off to find something else to do.

'I wonder what my allotment is looking like,' Jack said, heaving a clod of turf out of the nascent pit. 'Still, I don't suppose a couple of fallow years will hurt it.'

Geordie paused in his digging to shrug off his greatcoat.

'What's the point in wondering?' he asked, bundling up his coat and tossing it to one side. 'Leeks and potatoes, it's neither here nor there.'

'You've got to keep something from home in your thoughts,' Trevor said. 'You've got to carry *something* with you, otherwise it all gets too far away.'

'Not me.' Geordie kicked his spade into the ground. 'When I left, I left. If I get back, well that's a bonus. There'll be time enough to wonder and think when I'm on the troopship crossing the channel.'

'Onions, mostly,' Jack muttered to himself. 'Sometimes a stand of runners.'

The stuttering rattle of aero engines nibbled at the air. Charlie stopped work and scanned the sky for the source. Coming in from the west, a gaggle of five British scouts processed serenely towards the city. Benign roundels of red, white and blue decorated the cream-painted undersides of their wings. Below them, converging from a different angle, two larger aircraft lumbered along.

Percy followed Charlie's gaze upwards, leaning on his spade to watch as the fighters overflew them. The biplanes reached the centre of Arras and then wheeled tightly to starboard to escort the two other aircraft as they banked to fly a southerly route directly towards the front lines.

'What must it be like up there?' Charlie breathed. 'Flying through the air must be a marvellous thing.'

'It's a new age, Charlie, that's for sure,' Percy said. 'Imagine what they'll be able to do with those things when there's no longer a war to be fought.'

'I would love to be a pilot,' Charlie mused, following the scouts with his eyes as they receded into the grey distance. He switched his gaze back to Percy. '*Could* I ever become a pilot, do you think?'

'Volunteer,' Percy said, plunging his spade into the earth once more. 'They'll give you a physical, check your eyesight, and if you pass, they'll send you back to England to teach you how to fly.' He paused again in his work and gazed wistfully into the middle distance. 'Think of it,' he said. 'You'd be at home for the summer.'

'Oh, no,' Charlie said. 'I couldn't do that. It would be like running away. You'd think I was a coward.'

'Charlie, you're not much past being a boy.' Percy pulled out his cigarettes, lit one and breathed deeply on the smoke. 'Volunteer, lad. Take the chance of a few weeks out of this horrible French shit-hole. You might' – his eyes widened in mock amazement – 'find yourself a girlfriend.' He warmed to his theme. 'Oh, think of it' – he slipped off his helmet and held it over his heart – 'kissing her sweet, soft lips under the blossoming apple trees.'

'Stop it, Percy.' Charlie's cheeks reddened. 'Stop larking about.'

A truck ground to a halt next to the digging men. Two junior staff officers climbed out and walked back to the tailgate. One retrieved a sledgehammer, the other pulled out a sign covered by sacking. At a short distance from the marked-out pits, the second man held the sign upright as the first drove it into the ground with the hammer. The man with the hammer walked back to the truck and started the engine. The other man paused to regard the digging soldiers for a few moments, then pulled the sack covering from the sign to reveal the words *DEAD DUMP*, before following his companion.

Chapter 4

Wednesday, 21 March 1917 – Vert Galant

Claypole glanced around at his flight commanders as they finished eating breakfast.

'Gentlemen,' he began, 'I have two bits of rather chilling news.'

Faces tilted towards him in silent expectation.

'First, the quartermaster tells me that coffee stocks are running short. Apparently German submarines are causing mayhem amongst merchant vessels off the American coast and we're losing a lot of cargo.'

Stiles looked down into his mug with genuine pathos.

'Vicious bastards,' he muttered under his breath.

'Second, the wing commander is visiting front line squadrons today to deliver a personal briefing on the current situation.'

'Tarquin Beadle?' Hartley groaned. 'That despicable bugger-monkey?'

'*Lieutenant Colonel* Tarquin Beadle, yes.' Claypole glared at Hartley: 'Please don't be rude about the man. He's our bloody wing commander despite his recreational proclivities. You *will* respect his rank.'

'When's the old relic getting here?' Stiles swirled and sipped at his coffee like it was a fine wine.

'He's on his rounds now, so any time, I expect.'

Davenport put his hand up: 'Should I cancel my morning patrol, sir?'

'No. The war doesn't stop. Not even for Tarquin Beadle.'

Davenport stood, unable to hide his smile of relief, and bustled away to find his flying kit.

'So, it looks like you might be right, sir,' Mumford said quietly. 'Another spring offensive.'

'There's not much else it can be,' Claypole said. 'And it *would* be nice to get it over with and go home, albeit three Christmases late.'

Davenport waddled past the table in his leather flying suit and opened the door. A gust of frigid breeze blew across the floor and sucked a belch of white smoke from the stove's ill-fitting hotplate.

Davenport closed the farmhouse door and surveyed the sky. A hint of blue struggled to impose its influence on the grey, wintry dome. But the clouds sailed high; all-in-all, decent conditions for a jaunt up and down the lines.

He clumped down the steps and started towards the pilots' mess. Riggers were already dragging the Pups backwards into the centre of the field, a man on each wing and one either side of the tail, swivelling them to face the breeze. Four pilots waited for him in front of the mess hut, drawing to attention as he approached.

'At ease, gentlemen.' He looked from face to face. 'Not a bad day for an outing. We're on a routine patrol, so we'll keep it nice and simple. We'll stay over on our side and hope nothing untoward crops up to spoil the day. Right, let's go.'

From inside the mess, Benn watched the group disperse to their aircraft. Sucking hard on a cigarette, he blew the smoke against the glass, where it roiled like ripples in a pond. He crossed to the wall of silhouettes and sought out the pilots who were now starting their engines. Davenport, in the top row with the other flight commanders. Munnings and Clamp, he reached up and touched the faces as he found them, like an inquisitive cat taps the pieces on a chessboard. And Minton, the old hand from before the Somme offensive. His fingers lingered on Minton's brow as he glanced over to a table where the man's pipe and worn leather tobacco pouch awaited his return. Finally, Hector, one of the new boys. Hector had been rattled by the rapid demise of Cant and Griffiths, and the emotional decline of Morris following the loss of his friend, a weakness belied by the strong nose and jutting jaw of the man's paper profile.

The choke and roar of aero engines drew Benn back to the window and he watched the gaggle of Pups loft into the air and claw for altitude as they banked east. His eyes followed them as they wobbled away until their clattering faded into distant silence.

A different engine approached, a smoother, more fluid sound. Benn craned his neck to catch sight of a staff car drawing up in front of the farmhouse. A young orderly leapt from the front passenger side and opened the rear door. A tall, slim officer unfurled from the back seat, stretched his back and adjusted his jacket and belt.

'Oh, shit,' Benn murmured. 'Look who's about.'

Lieutenant Colonel Tarquin Beadle ascended the steps and opened the farmhouse door. A wave of fuggy warmth belched over him and chairs and boots clattered as Jackdaw Squadron's commanders sprung to attention.

'At ease, gentlemen' – Beadle narrowed his eyes in an unconvincing impersonation of a smile – 'please be seated.'

The orderly closed the door and stood next to it in stiff anticipation with the wing commander's briefcase clasped firmly with both hands.

'Would you like a coffee, sir?' Claypole asked. 'Or, I think there's some wine around the place somewhere.'

Beadle shook his head slightly, as if the suggestion was foolish: 'Let's get straight to business. I think that would be best.'

Beadle sat down at the head of the table and rubbed his hands together like a benefactor at an almsgiving.

'Things are changing, gentlemen. Indeed, they are changing with such drama and fortitude that I suspect we'll all be home for Christmas.'

Claypole and Mumford exchanged a look.

'There's going to be another big push,' the wing commander announced, holding out a hand in the direction of his orderly.

The man rummaged in the briefcase, pulled out a map and hurried it into the officer's outstretched palm.

'All top secret of course,' Beadle continued, eyeing each man in turn to reinforce that fact while he unfolded the map on the table. 'The infantry attack will be on a front starting at Vimy at the northern end, down through Arras and as far south as Bullecourt. There's some indication that German troops are already withdrawing in some sectors, probably shortening their line to concentrate resources. This makes it doubly important to keep a close eye on what the Hun is up to at all times.

'So, photo reconnaissance flights are our top priority. In fact, they are the *only* priority. Missions will be flown, re-flown and flown again until satisfactory photographic plates are delivered to the intelligence officers at HQ. Then, the next day, they'll be flown once more to see if anything has changed. This will be continued until the offensive begins, at which point the observer crews will switch to counter-battery control.'

Claypole leaned forward: 'Counter-battery control? What's that?'

Beadle pulled a sickly smile: '*That* is what will change the game in our favour. There'll be observer aircraft aloft throughout the infantry attack. As soon as they spot a German artillery piece opening up, they transmit the map reference by Morse code to a dedicated battery of our guns. They continue to circle the target and observe our shell-bursts, correct any error and walk the fire onto the German emplacement. Once on target, our gunners switch to gas shells and it will be curtains for another enemy gun crew. Which means the infantry can advance largely unmolested.'

'What's our part in this?' Claypole asked.

'Ah!' Beadle nodded sagely. 'It's fairly obvious our observer boys can't carry out these exacting tasks *and* defend themselves against enemy scouts. So, your task will be to fly in support of these missions and make sure that photo reconnaissance meets with minimal interference from the Germans.'

Claypole slumped back into his chair: 'Minimal interference?'

'Yes' – Beadle nodded as if he was confirming the price of a train ticket – 'your job, and that of fighter squadrons like yours, is to shoot down, or otherwise prevent from working, all enemy aircraft over your sector of the frontlines.'

'That's quite a task, sir,' Claypole said. 'We're up against the Albatros in this sector and some of the German pilots are very experienced. Sometimes the only sensible course of action is to withdraw and wait for a better opportunity the next day.'

Beadle chewed his lip for a moment. 'I have to emphasise that our reconnaissance objectives will be pursued with no heed to the cost,' he said. 'Even if your men are outnumbered by better pilots in better machines who hold a tactical advantage, it is their imperative duty to engage the enemy before they reach the observation aircraft, regardless of risk.' Beadle smiled broadly: 'We're fairly certain the Germans have fewer pilots than we do. So, your lads just have to kill one of theirs and they've done their bit. Mathematically, trading one for one will get us where we need to be.'

'Under these circumstances' – Claypole's voice held a tense edge – 'may I request that I be allowed to go on operational flights?'

'Certainly not, you know the regulations. We need our squadron commanders safe on the ground.'

'Sir' – Stiles spoke up – 'I have leave requested-'

'Not anymore,' Beadle interrupted 'All leave is cancelled for the foreseeable future.' He looked around their faces again as he folded the map. 'The offensive is provisionally set for Easter Sunday, gentlemen. There are an awful lot of photographs that need to be taken before then.'

Beadle folded the map, pushed his chair back and stood. The flight commanders all rose in unison.

'If there are no further questions, I'll be on my way. Busy times ahead.'

The orderly opened the door and followed the wing commander out. The four men in the room sat down and listened as the staff car pulled away.

Stiles shook his head and tutted: 'My missus will be livid.'

***

Claypole finished his lunch and pushed the plate away across the table. He wrinkled his nose against the last lingering vestige of Beadle's cologne, stood and retrieved his greatcoat. Wrapping a scarf around his neck, he stepped out onto the porch. The chill breeze smarted tears into his eyes. He brushed them away, pulled his scarf up over his nose and crossed the road to the airfield.

At the far end of the field three working parties laboured along the hedgerow, digging separate pits about forty feet apart. Men shovelled the spoil from each pit into hessian sacks and their comrades stacked the filled bags into a column next to the hole, kicking and slapping them into place to ensure a solid construction.

Claypole meandered towards the activity, stopping at a fair distance to avoid bringing the men to attention and interrupting their progress. Satisfied that his orders had been understood he retraced his steps. Lieutenant Minton stood alone outside the pilots' mess, his pipe smoke churning away in the breeze like fleeing phantoms as he watched the working parties with keen curiosity.

Claypole diverted towards him.

'Who's up?' he called.

Minton jerked to attention. 'Captain Hartley's flight, sir.'

'Right, when they're down, I want everyone assembled in the mess. Then come and get me.'

Minton watched his squadron commander stride away. Then, lifting his pipe back to his mouth, he returned his gaze to the growing stacks by the hedge.

***

Claypole stood in front of the assembled pilots like a headmaster, clasping his hands before him. The four flight commanders sat straight-backed on wooden chairs behind him, lending a quiet authority to his presence. Nonetheless, a crackle of tension buzzed in the air.

'I imagine you've been expecting things to liven up sooner or later' – Claypole's firm voice projected into the room – 'and one or two of you who were with Jackdaw at the end of last summer will not be surprised that another offensive is indeed being planned. Nor will you be surprised that our given task is to deny the enemy the ability to operate over the lines.'

Someone emitted a low groan of despair that Claypole chose to ignore.

'To achieve this, the number of routine patrols per day will be doubled, and every patrol will be undertaken with aggressive commitment. You will engage any and all German scouts you see over the lines at any and every opportunity. Flights not on routine patrol will stand ready for escort duties with the reconnaissance squadrons. It is these observation and photography flights that we are tasked to protect by making the air over the lines untenable for the Germans and by close escort support, when requested, for the aircraft making the observations.

'You have no doubt seen the firing butts under construction at the far end of the aerodrome. As soon as I've finished here, we start checking and aligning the guns, three planes at a time. You'll stand a better chance of bringing the Hun down if your bullets are going where your sights are suggesting they might be.

'And from now on, each pilot will assemble and prepare their own ammunition belts. If you lavish enough tender care on them, you won't have to worry about jamming in the breeches. Are there any questions?'

The room stayed silent.

Claypole turned to his flight commanders: 'Hartley, you'll fly the dawn patrol, so get your Pups to the firing range and start working on them immediately. Decide amongst yourselves who takes the other slots. If you take casualties, sequester pilots from another flight for your next patrol. Try to make sure no-one does two runs in a row.' A terse smile creased his face. 'Carry on gentlemen.'

Everyone stood as Claypole left the mess. Silence hung over them for long moments as the two groups looked at each other through the lens of their new reality.

Outside, Claypole walked stiffly back to the farmhouse, the frustrated desire to fly and fight burned like a knot of colic in his guts.

Chapter 5

Thursday, 22 March 1917

Short chops of machine gun fire crackled across the field, splitting the icy dawn with their brittle cacophony. Three Sopwith Pups sat line abreast, their tails jacked up on wooden tripods to bring their bodies into the horizontal. Before them, the tattered hessian on the butts flapped around the circular canvas marker pegged to their face. At the side of each butt, a spotter crouched, huddling low, steel helmet strapped firmly to his head, popping up and calling corrections after each burst. Teetering on a step ladder and leaning under the top wing, a spanner-wielding armourer waited for the call before leaning through the spars and rigging to make adjustments to the gun mountings.

Captain Hartley strode towards his pilots, huddled in the grey cold outside the mess. They came to what passed for attention in their thick fleece flying suits.

'At ease.' Hartley's breath swirled white around his head as he regarded the men. 'I want you to remember what Major Claypole said at yesterday's briefing. Today we fight like bulldogs. We are seeking nothing short of the kill. If the Hun comes looking for trouble, it's our job to make sure he doesn't get home.' He sniffed hard against a dribbling nostril. 'But also remember to stick together. Take your lead from me and avoid dangerous freelancing. Let's go.'

Hartley trudged out towards his fighter. His pilots fanned out behind him, each man heading for his own aircraft. The solidity of the rough, frozen ground jolted Hartley's knee-joints. A sudden thrill of realisation gripped his vitals; these could be his last steps. He suppressed the thought. What if they were? Today or tomorrow, what would be the difference?

He reached his machine and clambered onto the port wing.

'All primed and ready, sir.' The rigger standing on the other wing root helped him into the cockpit and then jumped to the ground.

Trotting round to the front of the fighter, the man stopped and waited. Hartley switched on the magnetos, engaged the starter and waved his hand. The rigger reached up to grab the tip of the highest blade and flipped the propeller down and around, using his momentum to pirouette his body away from the aircraft. The engine coughed into life, splitting the damp morning apart with its dry roar. The rigger ducked down and grabbed a rope from the grass. Without looking back, he walked away with the chocks from Hartley's wheels bouncing after him, dragged like reluctant puppies at the end of the cords he grasped.

Hartley's aircraft rolled forward and gathered speed, his booted foot tapping right rudder to keep the craft in line against the engine's torque. The tail lifted first, then the body of the trim biplane soared off the ground. Hartley accelerated into a straight and shallow climb while his flight assembled around him, then banked north-west and pulled into a steeper ascent, buying altitude with speed over friendly territory.

Below them, bang on time, a flight of three BE2s lumbered eastwards; the mission they were detailed to escort. Hartley waggled his wings and banked starboard into an easterly heading that matched that of the reconnaissance craft. The two Pups on the outside of the turn splayed out, losing height in their effort to keep pace. Hartley watched them stagger back into place over the course of several minutes, easier prey had they been nearer the hunters' territory.

Ahead, emerging under the strengthening light, parallel ribbons of brown and grey marked the trenches and wire of the frontline, like the ragged border of a huge dull carpet. This side of the lines, darker crescents of brown marked out fresh earthworks. Around some of these emplacements, long fingers of shadow stretched across the ground, cast by dumps of shells. Some of the pits stood empty, awaiting the arrival of more artillery.

The gun batteries drifted away beneath the flight, giving way to a churned landscape scarred by meandering communication trenches. A few invisible figures, betrayed by their dawn-lit shadows, flowed into these narrow thoroughfares from the pockmarked hinterland. Beyond this, heading east, there was no discernible sign of life or movement despite the thousands of men that found their home in the gashed soil.

Hartley crossed over no man's land at nine thousand feet. He glanced down to the BE2s, expecting them to begin their photo run along the German lines, but they continued eastwards. Evidently their objective was deeper into enemy territory.

Ahead, in otherwise pristine German-held territory, the grey dawn was blackened by columns of smoke curling into the sky. Hartley scanned left and right, picking out more conflagrations in the distance, spewing fumes and sparks into the morning air.

'*Whump!*

The blast wave jolted his aircraft and his engine coughed in protest. A second later his Pup flew through the ball of white smoke. More anti-aircraft shells burst ahead of the flight and Hartley waved his hand over his head, banked to starboard and increased speed. He glanced over each shoulder to see the others tilting their wings in unison. A line of explosions cut the air close on the port side, whining fragments spinning through space around the formation. He waved his arm again, turned slightly to port and increased speed once more.

Hartley's buttocks tensed against the expectation of sudden mutilation and he fought the urge to look down, to seek out the muzzle flash that hurled his fate skywards.

A group of blasts peppered the sky well behind on the starboard quarter. They were through! Hartley glanced to each side; his flight remained intact. But the tension didn't ease as they droned further eastward, above and now slightly ahead of their charges.

Hartley scanned the sky in front, a low bank of clouds skulked across the lightening grey heavens. He shuffled in his seat to peer around his cowling to search for climbing adversaries. A movement caught his eye, and he squinted through the ground haze to discern a snaking column of soldiers. He stared at the mass of men, searching for a clue that would tell him their direction of travel.

Something smacked into his port upper-wingtip. He wrenched his head around to see tracer splay away from his wing and cone onto the Pup next to him. Thick splinters of wooden strut and tattered canvas spun away in the slipstream as the other scout's port wing collapsed and folded flat against the fuselage. Lift from the intact starboard wings lurched the plane sideways, twisting it into the fighter on its port side. The propeller scythed into the other's cockpit, breaking and bending the craft's body and locking the wrecked machines together to spiral down in a terminal embrace.

Hartley kicked his rudder and banked steeply to his left, into the space left by his fallen comrades. The dark shapes of the attacking fighters flashed over his head. Craning his neck backwards, he watched the enemy circus bank left and dive in a long curve towards the east. Hauling around in a full circle he levelled out to give chase, his turn putting him way behind his retreating quarry.

The Germans fanned out, splitting up for self-preservation. Hartley picked one and dipped his nose towards it. He lined his sights up slightly above the fleeing Albatros and squeezed out a dozen rounds. He marked the tracer's path, adjusted and fired another burst. Smiling in satisfaction as the biplane ahead of him began weaving from side to side to evade the bullets, Hartley barrelled on, straight and level, gaining ground rapidly. He checked the sky around him. The other Germans were all running east, now far ahead of their comrade. The other two Pups, maintaining station over the BE2s, were the only other fighters aloft.

The German realised the growing danger in which he'd become embroiled and pulled into a climbing turn. Hartley anticipated the change in direction, pulled and held the trigger, and banked into the same trajectory, leading his enemy by a few degrees. The Albatros edged into the bullet stream, strikes dancing on the engine cowling and working backwards. When they reached the cockpit, Hartley increased his turn to keep them there. The pilot's head and shoulders splashed gouts of red gore that plumed backwards in the propeller wash and splattered across the fuselage behind the cockpit.

Hartley pulled away from his plummeting kill and banked west, towards the remnants of his flight, the retreating reconnaissance planes and the safety of British territory.

***

The three biplanes dropped into a circuit of Vert Galant and Hartley led them down to land on the rough grass, swinging off the landing strip and rolling to a halt outside the canvas hangars at the field's edge. Hartley shut off his engine and stared through the propeller arc as it slowed to a faltering stop. He jumped at the sudden rattle of machine gun fire from the firing range. Composing himself, he pulled off his flying gauntlets and undid his lap strap.

A rigger appeared by the wing root.

'Everything alright with the ship, sir?' he asked.

Hartley pointed to the port wing-tips as he climbed down to the grass: 'I'm sure I took some hits on the wing' – the two men walked out to examine the shredded canvas – 'and we flew through some Archie on the way out, so give everything a once-over, would you?'

'Two missing?' Claypole's voice catapulted the rigger to attention.

Hartley turned and pulled off his leather helmet.

'Yes, sir. They dived on us from out of the clouds, four or maybe five of them. They hit us and ran away. It certainly didn't look like they wanted to stick around and fight us, and they completely ignored the recon boys. I chased one of them down and finished him.'

'Who did we lose?'

'McGarry and Humphrey. One lost a wing and ploughed into the other. It was carnage.'

'That's a shame. McGarry was a good man.' Claypole turned and walked away. Hartley hurried after him.

'I saw German infantry retreating in some numbers, and they're burning things as they go,' Hartley said.

Claypole looked across at him through narrowed eyelids: 'Burning things?'

'I suppose they're burning villages,' Hartley said.

'Villages?'

'They were very big fires, sir, well outside the range of our artillery.'

'Bastards,' Claypole spat. 'Absolute bottom-drawer bastards.' He stomped a few paces in silence. 'Anyway, how was the gun alignment?'

'Very good, sir. My bullets went exactly where I wanted them to go.'

***

Benn watched through the window as Claypole and Hartley walk past on their way to the farmhouse. The mess door opened admitting Cobbit and Harkin. They trudged over to a bench to get out of their flying kit. Benn's eyes followed them across the room, a deep frown creasing his forehead. He looked from Cobbit to Harkin and back, then stood and walked slowly to the silhouette wall. It took him a few moments to find the two faces he sought. He removed them tenderly and held them together in his hand for a few seconds. He turned abruptly, opened the stove door and laid the silhouettes on the glowing embers. The paper curled, crisped and burst into flames. Benn smiled and closed the door.

Saturday, 24 March 1917

'Are you alright?' Potter looked across the trellis workbench at Morris: 'You look a bit pale.'

Morris kept his eyes fixed on the ammunition belt he was assembling.

'I'll be alright,' he said. 'It's just an awfully strange situation to be in.'

Platt stepped away from his chair to warm his fingers over a nearby brazier.

'What makes it any stranger for you?' he asked over his shoulder.

Morris stopped fiddling with bullets and leaned heavily on the bench.

'I was planning to become a priest,' Morris explained. 'I had a place lined up in Cambridge to study theology.'

'What changed the plan?' Potter returned to the table.

'One of the ladies in our church pinned a white feather on my lapel,' Morris said. 'She did it in front of the whole congregation while we were waiting for the sacrament.'

Potter whistled through his teeth: 'Brassy!'

'I had to volunteer immediately,' Morris said. 'There was nothing else I could do.'

Platt paused in his work and joined the conversation.

'Why the RFC?' he asked.

Morris smiled in spite of himself: 'I didn't think I'd get shot at quite so much in an aeroplane.'

Potter stifled a laugh.

'Still' – Platt shot a sideways glare at his friend – 'I'm sure having a strong faith makes everything a bit less scary.'

'No' – Morris' voice threatened to crack – 'I'm bloody terrified. And the worst thing is, I don't know if it comes from a fear of death or a love of life.' He looked up with nascent tears bulging in his eyes. 'And here I am weaving bullets together that I know I can't in all conscience fire at another man.'

Platt regarded the other man with a sick mixture of empathy and horror.

'You have to fight when commanded to do so, Morris,' he hissed. 'If you don't, they'll-'

'At ease, lads.' Captain Stiles arrived at the bench, dirty white overalls covering his uniform, a khaki muffler coiled around his neck. 'Space for a small one?'

The men watched in quiet confusion as Stiles took a handful of clips and a handful of bullets from the boxes on the end of the bench and began piecing them together.

'Morning, sir,' Platt said. 'We hadn't imagined that Major Claypole included flight commanders in his order.'

Stiles looked up briefly: 'No. I don't imagine he did either. But if building your own ammunition belt means it's less likely to jam, I can see no reason why I should forego the advantage.'

The men worked without speaking for long moments, the silence only broken by Morris' occasional sniffles.

Platt stilled his hands again.

'Listen,' he said. 'Can you hear an engine?'

The others paused and cocked their heads. The grumbling grind of an aero engine grew louder.

'That's odd,' Stiles mumbled. 'Mumford's flight took off only ten minutes ago.' He stood up and drifted to the hangar entrance, Platt trailing in his wake. Both men scanned the sky.

'There!' Platt called, pointing to the east of the field. 'It looks like a Frenchie.'

The silver biplane overflew the field and banked into an untidy circuit, its blue, white and red tailplane strident against the backdrop of wintry clouds.

'Go and fetch Major Claypole.' Stiles slapped Platt's shoulder: 'Go!'

Platt ran towards the farmhouse and Stiles wandered out into the field, keeping his eye on the wobbling aircraft as it circled, searching for an approach line that faced the breeze. Stiles watched it yaw, sideslip and jerk back to level flight. Then it dipped its nose and swooped into a landing gradient.

Stiles turned at the sound of pounding boots; Claypole and Platt lurched to a halt next to him.

'What's his game?' Claypole panted out his question.

'Well, he's either a terrible pilot, or he's injured,' Stiles said.

Riggers and armourers came to the open entrances of the hangars, watching the French fighter's antics with detached interest.

The French plane bounced once on the grass, stalled and dropped heavily to the ground, weaving as it slowed to a halt.

The three men trotted towards the stationary craft and Stiles heaved himself up onto the port wing, grasping the cockpit edge and pulling himself forward to look at the cockpit's occupant. The pilot's head lolled like a man awakening from a doze and he fixed his bleary gaze on Stiles.

'Ma jambe…' he muttered.

'Do you speak English, son?' Stiles raised his voice against the idling engine.

'Ma jambe.' The Frenchman's dull eyes implored the face in front of him. 'Coups de feu… d'en bas…'

Stiles turned to find the fuel cocks and silence the engine. He recoiled instinctively; the instrument panel dripped red with blood, splashed up from below. He looked down at the pilot's legs. His fleece flying suit was ripped and stained crimson, and the man's fist was pushed into his groin in an attempt to stem the flow of blood. As he watched, the pilot's arm relaxed, his fist rolled away from his groin and a turgid fountain pulsed from the revealed wound, once, twice, then stopped.

'He's dead,' Claypole said, leaning over from the starboard wing. 'The fuel cocks' – he pointed – 'there and there. Shut them off.'

'Yes, sir.' Stiles threw the levers, fingers sliding on the slick, congealing blood.

'There's blood dripping out of the bullet holes under the cockpit' – Claypole squinted along the fuselage and across the wings – 'but other than that, this ship looks in fine condition.'

Stiles stared aghast at his squadron commander as the man cast a studious gaze across the instrument panel, chewing his lip in concentration.

'It all looks fairly standard,' Claypole murmured. 'Nothing to cause any nasty surprises.'

He glanced at the pallid pilot and straightened his back.

'Platt!' he called out, beckoning at the man loitering by the tail of the aircraft. 'Help Captain Stiles get the Frenchie out.'

Stiles shook his head in quiet dismay, but reached down to unhitch the pilot's lap-belt. He squirmed his hands under the man's arms, braced, and pulled the body up and out of the cockpit. He stepped backwards onto the grass and Platt took hold of the dead man's ankles, avoiding contact with the blood-drenched thighs and crotch. They laid the pilot gently on the grass and Stiles crossed the man's arms over his chest and closed the glazing eyes.

'My riggers!' Claypole's bellow rang across the field. 'Get over here… Now!'

Two men detached from the group loitering in the hangar entrance and jogged across the grass towards the silver aircraft. While he waited, Claypole walked around to the front of the plane, running his gloved hand over the polished metal of its cowling. The riggers arrived and snapped to attention.

'Right.' Claypole beckoned them to walk with him back around to the rear edge of the wing. 'I want the cockpit hosed clean and all the control lines checked. Then patch up the bullet holes on the underside. Check the main spar and give the engine a once-over.' He paused and peered at each rigger in turn to ensure they'd understood.

'Yes, sir,' one of them said.

Claypole pointed at the tailplane with its Tricolour marking and serial number.

'I want that painted out in black and the roundels re-done to British colours,' he said. 'Once that's complete, this aeroplane must be kept in the hangar under tarpaulin, and I am the *only* – he waggled his finger at them to emphasise the point – '*only* one that flies it.'

The riggers grabbed the tail of the craft, dragging it backwards towards the hangar, calling across the field for help.

Claypole sauntered over to where Stiles and Platt were standing by the body, a broad smile splitting his face.

'A Nieuport 17,' he purred. 'It's what the Hun copied to make the Albatros. Isn't it beautiful? What a gift!'

Stiles frowned: 'Surely, when they come to collect the body, they'll want to take the aeroplane as well.'

'They won't be collecting the body.' Claypole caught and held the other man's eye. 'We won't be needing three target butts anymore.' He pointed at the firing range. 'Put him in one of the pits and dismantle the butt to cover him.'

'You can't do that,' Stiles spluttered. 'He has family…'

'Harry' – Claypole laid his hand on the other man's shoulder – 'it's not as if it will be the first unmarked grave in France. And' – his voice hardened – 'I *will* have that Nieuport.'

Stiles shrugged off his commander's hand and stalked away towards the farmhouse.

Chapter 6

Monday, 26 March 1917

Mumford jiggled the bacon one last time and scraped the pan's contents onto his plate. Sitting down at the table, he glanced around. 'Where's the major?'

'He's out in the hangar,' Davenport replied. 'Mooning over that French fighter.'

'I can't say I blame him' – Mumford tore a chunk of dark bread from the loaf in the centre of the table – 'it is a thing of some loveliness. But what's he planning to do with it?'

'It seems,' Stiles said, 'he intends to fly it into combat.'

A moment of shocked silence hung over the table.

'That's not funny, Harry,' Davenport admonished. 'That would be against regulations. He'd end up on a charge.'

'I suspect that the disrespectful treatment of an ally's fallen pilot would put him on a charge as well,' Stiles said. 'But that didn't stop him hiding the Frenchman's corpse under a pile of sandbags.'

Silence dropped again and Davenport frowned his unease into space.

'We've lost four men in the past week' – Mumford's voice was steady and thoughtful – 'half the replacements we received are already dead. Hartley's up there now with two pilots from my flight. They'll have to go up with me later as well. We've got a big job on, and Claypole's a damned good fighter pilot. It makes no sense to ground him just because he's the squadron commander.'

Davenport's frown relaxed: 'What price being squadron commander anyway, when Beadle can waltz in and throw your squadron tactics out the window?' he said. 'I reckon, with Claypole in the air, I've got a slightly better chance of making it through.'

Stiles looked at the other two men. He lacked the energy to stay angry. The core of indignation he had lodged in his breast when he awoke that morning was subsumed under what he feared might become a bottomless capacity for sadness.

***

Benn flew next to Higgins on the starboard side of the formation as it droned north above a pair of photo reconnaissance BE2s. Their vector placed him closest to any attacking Germans diving in from the east, and this lurking vulnerability added to the unease he felt at being seconded into Hartley's flight. Hartley was an officer he didn't know well but instinctively disliked; a man tenacious enough to have already scored two victories, yet self-possessed enough not to brag about them.

Benn surveyed the German lines rolling by beneath them, sparsely decorated by the occasional burst of a British shell. But something was missing; everything looked somehow flatter, less alive. It struck him… there were no muzzle flashes from the trenches; no-one was firing at them. Intrigued, he squinted hard against the tearing prop-wash, probing the ground for any movement, any fluid shadow.

A multi-coloured shape flashed through his line of sight, a burst of blue and green. Benn jolted his severed attention away from the ground. Another Albatros sliced westwards tight below him, its guns spouting vivid yellow tongues of flame through its propeller.

'Shit!' Benn waggled his wings in an attempt to get his leader's attention and then side-slipped to port, under Higgins, diving after the attackers.

Three German scouts in line astern peppered the rearmost BE2 in a beam attack, each pulling up over the wallowing plane and banking starboard to circle onto the second. The British reconnaissance plane blossomed with fire that licked out from its engine and bannered along the fuselage. The aircraft nosed into a shallow dive, trailing thick white smoke in a lazy downward curve. As it drew near to the ground, the burning pilot levelled out in a desperate bid to crash-land, but the coiled wire snagged the wheels and somersaulted the disintegrating aircraft through the mud like a flame-flared Catherine wheel.

Benn tightened his turn to put himself between the enemy fighters and the remaining reconnaissance plane. The first two shied away from him and dived eastwards. The third was slow to see him and banked away late. Benn dropped onto his tail and fought to match the jinking swerves of his fleeing opponent.

The air swelled next to Benn, pushing him to port. A roar of redoubled engine noise and a black shape on the edge of his vision accompanied a jolt through the airframe and he looked across in shock at the face of his flight leader, barely two dozen feet away.

Their wingtips hit, jostled and creased. Benn pulled away to port, Hartley banked in the other direction. The wings disentangled and ragged shreds of canvas twirled away in their slipstreams.

Benn pulled the turn until he faced west, terrified the damage would bring him down again in no man's land. But his Pup flew on, pulling towards the damaged wing, but manageable. Benn scanned the heavens. Hartley was still airborne, over on his starboard side, also heading west. Behind him, the sky was mercifully empty. Ahead, Higgins and the other two Pups in the flight umbrellaed the retreating BE2. In their wake, the smoke from the burning wreckage of the other reconnaissance plane coiled into the frigid dawn air.

Benn flew with his right knee braced against the stick, but the starboard planes still bucked like unruly stallions against his controlling pressure. Fearful of losing that control, Benn flew well wide and slightly behind the others, a lamb to slaughter should a German scout be chasing them. The dread tickled the nape of his neck and he clenched his teeth against its seduction.

Hartley flew ahead and the others took formation behind him, allowing a respectful distance for his erratic flightpath.

The outline of Vert Galant coalesced from the haze like the outstretched palms of a beseeching saviour and Hartley dropped towards the field with no preamble. Benn watched the others bank for a circuit and, with a surge of relief, dropped his nose to follow his leader in to land. Mindful that a stall would likely flip him, he kept up revs on his approach and touched down slightly fast. The Pup bounced, resettled and rattled across the rough grass, passing Hartley's already stationary aircraft before pirouetting to a halt.

Benn shut off the fuel taps and the wooden propeller clanked to a halt. The metal of the hot engine ticked and wheezed in the frigid air, mirroring Benn's own sigh of relief. He climbed out of the cockpit and jumped to the grass, the muscles in his right thigh trembling on the point of cramp.

'What the bloody hell are you playing at?' Hartley stalked up to him, breath billowing wreaths of condensation that swathed his fury.

Benn snapped to attention, wincing at the stiffness in his leg.

'Following orders, sir,' he answered. 'Flying aggressively against an enemy scout.'

'Did you not see *me*?' Hartley's voice rose several tones.

'No, sir.' The obvious return question went unasked, but blazed silently in Benn's eyes.

Hartley turned on his heel and strode towards the hangars. Behind him, the three other Pups drifted down towards the field, taking lines between and around the haphazardly parked aircraft on the landing strip.

The warmer air inside the hanger, fed by numerous braziers glowing in the gloom, pricked sweat into Hartley's armpits. He cast his eyes about for his rigger, eventually lighting on Claypole, tinkering with bracing wires on the French fighter's fuselage. He closed the distance between them.

'Sir?' he said. 'May I have a word?'

Claypole straightened and turned.

'Ah, Hartley,' he said 'How was the patrol?'

'Very nearly disastrous, but we all got back in the end,' Hartley answered. 'We lost one of the reconnaissance planes to some German scouts that we were' – he chewed on his words – 'unable to engage.'

'Oh' – Claypole laid his spanner on the Nieuport's tailplane – 'HQ are expecting losses. You shouldn't let it disturb you too much.'

'We're wasting our guns,' Hartley said. 'That's what disturbs me.'

Claypole stayed silent, raising an eyebrow to invite expansion.

'Flying alongside the spotters in a nice tidy formation is the worst way of protecting them,' Hartley continued. 'We were well above them this morning and the Germans cut in underneath us. If we fly at the same altitude, they simply dive through us. Flying close escort only makes the Hun's target bigger.'

Claypole nodded: 'I see your point. But flying alongside them makes the photo-boys feel safer.'

'What's the point of them feeling safer if we can't stop an Albatros cruising past us and lighting them on fire?' Hartley said. 'In truth, once the Hun gets that close, the observers' guns are a better defence than we are.'

'What are you suggesting?' Claypole asked.

'We need to catch the Hun circus at their airfield,' Hartley said. 'When they're taking off or landing, or better still, when they're lined up on the ground. We need to stop them ever laying eyes on our recon planes.'

Claypole picked up the spanner, hefted it in his hand and turned back to the silver fuselage.

'I'll send a memo to Beadle,' he said quietly, testing the tension of a wire with his free hand.

'When you do, would you also point out that the poor bloody recon boys are risking their lives photographing empty trenches.' Hartley turned away and went in search of his rigger.

***

Stiles stood at the farmhouse window watching Davenport's flight start up their engines in the grey mid-morning light. The stove door stood open to better heat the room and a hearty fire chuckled in the grate. But Stiles stood with his greatcoat buttoned to the neck. The solace of warmth eluded him; his flesh was ingrained with a creeping, involuntary coldness.

One by one the Pups waggled and yawed into the stiff westerly breeze, hauling away from the field, their outlines blurring into the wintry haze.

'What were Davenport's orders?' he asked over his shoulder.

Mumford looked up from his newspaper.

'Escorting photo reconnaissance again,' he said. 'Fritz doing a bunk has put HQ into a bit of a panic. Personally, I reckon it has to be a good sign. Maybe they're ready to negotiate a ceasefire. Maybe there won't be any need for another offensive.'

Stiles strained his eyes to hold sight of the airborne Pups as they banked away towards the east.

'A tactical withdrawal is never a good sign.' His voice sounded morose in his own ears. 'Whenever the enemy chooses to fall back of his own accord, under no immediate pressure, you can be fairly sure he considers his new location to be a better place from which to kill you than the one he's just left. Lord only knows what horrors they've put in place for our infantry along their new lines. I sincerely doubt our lads are in for a happy Easter.'

'Oh.' Mumford folded his paper into his lap. 'I hadn't thought of it like that.'

A flurry of movement by the hangars caught Harry's eye. A black tail edged out of the cavernous door and into the wan daylight, one man either side dragging it backwards across the grass. Stepped wings followed their silver fuselage with two men on each leading edge pushing the glistening Nieuport out towards the landing strip. Directing the groundcrew, a figure dressed in sheepskin flying gear pointed and gesticulated.

'It's looks like Jackdaw's unofficial supplementary air force is about to take to the air,' Stiles said.

Mumford came to stand next to Stiles at the window.

'He's a tenacious little bastard, isn't he?' he said.

57

'Without question,' Stiles agreed. 'But what happens to us if he doesn't come back?'

'I suppose they'll put you in command,' Mumford said. 'What with you being the oldest.'

'We'd all be on a charge for letting him do this in the first place,' Stiles muttered.

'Well' – Mumford turned away from the window – 'let's hope he comes back, then.'

***

The Nieuport skittered due east across the landscape, low, fast and full of slippery intent, like a dogfish skimming the seabed, alive and hungry. Claypole hunched in the cockpit, nerves thrumming with the exhilaration of speed and the seductive potency of the war machine he wielded. Approaching the scarred gash of no man's land, he dipped his wing to get a better view. A few upturned faces flashed by in the British trenches and a stretcher team ducked in apprehension, setting their lifeless burden down in readiness for flight. A few muzzle flashes sparkled beneath him, pulling a wry smile onto his face. Three seconds later he vaulted the German wire and hammered over the frozen mud of their deserted dugouts.

Easing the nose up, Claypole bent to view the map tied onto his thigh with parcel-string, flattening its flapping edges with his left hand. Behind the abandoned German line, the countryside recovered its vitality. But this transformation was marred by the ruins of farms and villages that still curled hazy smoke skywards from smouldering roof beams. Claypole meandered across the fields until he came across a lane heading east. He settled in to follow it, hoping to encounter some martial traffic, but it stretched away, deserted.

A flicker of movement against the clouds caught his eye. Up on his port quarter, three brightly painted biplanes cruised eastwards, seemingly unaware of his presence below them. Claypole crabbed across the space separating him from the formation and slotted in beneath their tails. Large black crosses corralled inside bright white squares decorated the underside of their wings; his first close-up view of the newest Albatros.

Safe in their blind spot, Claypole studied the rearmost of his three enemies, calculating where on the underside the cockpit floor might be and fixing his gaze on that spot. Easing back on the stick he waited for the ring-and-bead sight to line up and squeezed a short burst of fire. The canvas underside of his adversary shredded with a tight group of holes and the aircraft wallowed slightly. Claypole snapped another, longer burst and banked sharply to port, diving away to the west. Craning his neck over his shoulder he saw the first two biplanes in the enemy flight cruise on unperturbed, while his target lost height, riding its dead pilot towards the ground.

***

Benn sat in a battered leather armchair against the wall. His right knee cap twitched with involuntary spasm and he watched it in fascination, licking his lips like a cat watching a mousehole.

Minton sat down on the stool next to him, his cheeks smirched with oily grime from his recent patrol.

'How are you, lad?' he asked quietly.

Benn's gaze switched to Minton's face, but his expression remained unchanged.

'Concerned,' he intoned. 'Yes. A bit worried.' His eyes drifted back to his oscillating patella. 'I have to go up again this afternoon, because' – his gaze darted up to the silhouette wall – 'people don't come back.' He looked at Minton again, his sharp features softening. 'I nearly didn't come back.'

Minton rubbed tobacco in his cupped left hand, releasing its woody aroma to drift between the two men.

'But you did come back' – he pulled his pipe from his pocket and scooped the walnut-brown shreds into its bowl – 'and you'll continue to do so. You're a good pilot.'

'That Frenchman was a good pilot,' Benn hissed. 'He managed to land with his guts on the floor. It takes a damn good pilot to pull that one off.'

The door swung open and Captain Mumford's head appeared. 'My flight, ready in ten minutes.'

Benn stiffened, his right hand slid down his thigh and clutched his knee to stillness.

Minton lit his pipe, sucking the dancing flame down into the glowing tobacco. 'Off you go, lad,' he said. 'I'll see you later.'

Chapter 7

Wednesday, 28 March 1917

Morris stared into the ashen dome that stretched above the four Pups as they climbed east towards the frontlines. In places where the clouds were stretched thinner by high altitude winds, the hard slate complexion of the firmament was softened to pearly iridescence by the sun they obscured, creating concavities of light like gleaming oyster shells set into the barren sky. He switched his disconsolate gaze to Stiles at the head of the formation, watching him scan ahead in search of any trouble the flight could cause. His chilled muscles twitched as his apprehension mounted to queasy fear.

Stiles waved a hand above his head and pointed down to where white puffs of anti-aircraft fire bunched in the air above the British communication trenches. The leader's Pup dipped into a dive, but Morris paused, waiting until Platt and Potter followed before he pushed his nose down to join the descent.

Focussing where the shell-bursts drifted, he saw one, then another dun shape traversing parallel to the British wire. Black crosses on the top of their wings marked them as an enemy reconnaissance flight. Morris fishtailed and the distance between him and his companions widened; he could be present but remain uninvolved.

The two lumbering biplanes spotted their attackers and dived away over no man's land towards home. Observers in their rear nacelles opened up with defensive fire, sending tracers whirling through the sky, ahead and wide of their pursuers.

Stiles started shooting, closely followed by both Platt and Potter. Pennants of gun smoke peeled away in their slipstreams as burst after burst of machine gun fire reached out to the fleeing enemy. Morris gazed in agonised empathy at the rearmost German biplane as a nodule of flame flickered around the pilot, evolving quickly from warm orange to intense yellow. Fingers of flame soon lashed along the fuselage, reaching out for the observer.

Stiles led the flight over and past the stricken aircraft, climbing for a second pass. Morris cranked his head sideways in time to see the observer scramble from his seat and tip over the edge of the burning craft, tumbling head over feet through space towards the barren earth.

Suddenly something slashed through the canvas of his starboard wing, close by the fuselage. Morris jerked his head around, staring in confusion at the damage. The air behind his head hissed with malice and holes ripped across the fuselage behind his cockpit. A swelling roar filled his ears and a huge, predatory shape dropped past his nose. Morris glanced across into the face of murder as the German banked past his portside, curving and climbing to get behind him.

Morris snatched his eyes away to search out the compass on his instrument panel, pushing the stick to the left, dragging the luminous green 'W' around towards the needle. The Pup wallowed back to level flight and Morris rocked forwards and backwards in his seat, willing more speed from his aircraft. A shout escaped his throat as tracer whipped past, slicing rents along his port wing, hacking splinters from the struts and stitching a line towards the cockpit. Morris lurched the plane away from the bullet strikes and the attacking Albatros roared past, bottoming out of its dive and banking again. Morris stared aghast as the German fighter filled his gunsight and hung like a bloated sacrifice, helpless in front of his muzzle for long seconds.

The blast of the German's propwash cuffed his face as the Albatros skewed away from his nose. Morris choked back his sobs, hanging his life on the hope that his harrier would baulk at flying too deep into British territory. Bullets zipped past his right ear, lacerated the wing above his head and dipped to carve chunks of wood and glass out of his polished instrument panel.

'*There were two!*'

Instinctively Morris hauled back on the stick, twisting his neck to behold his tormentors. The Pup zoomed into the vertical, dragging its fuselage through a bullet stream that ripped canvas from its tail. The craft staggered into a loop, inverted and on the point of stall. The grasping fingers of gravity plucked at the panicking pilot's shoulders. Morris stiffened his body, bracing his legs against the cockpit sides and inadvertently pushed his left foot on the rudder. The Pup swooned into a sideslip that exaggerated into a spin as the machine dropped from the sky. Pressed into his seat, Morris started at explosions bursting in the space through which he dropped. He struggled against the whirling dizziness to think of what to do that might keep him alive. Something struck his knee. He looked down to see the stick flailing from side to side. He reached out to grab it. Tension and force fed from the plane through his arms and into his pounding chest. Instinctively he centred the stick and kicked at the rudder. The Sopwith lurched out of its spin and stalled. Morris let the nose tilt down to steal some speed from his meagre store of altitude, then pulled out of the dive barely two-hundred feet above the ground.

He looked up to see the two German scouts retreating, surrounded by the anti-aircraft bursts through which he had fallen. Flying straight and level, momentarily heedless of his direction or destination, he reached out his gloved hand to touch the chewed and ragged edge of his cockpit and the splintered wood of the instrument panel. Hot bile burned in his throat and tears stung his eyes as he gently banked his ripped and tattered aircraft westwards for Vert Galant.

***

Stiles saw the shape moving across the landscape below them and breathed a sigh of relief as he recognised it to be a Pup. He stayed above it as their courses converged and watched it set down at the airfield. Then he, Platt and Potter dropped down to the grass, engines spluttering as they slowed to a stop.

Stiles looked across at the errant Pup as he clambered out of his own fighter. Several men were gathered around the wings, but Morris sat unmoving in his cockpit. Stiles jumped to the grass and strode across, pulling off his helmet and stocking.

'Good grief,' he breathed to himself as the extent of damage the Pup carried became apparent. 'Is he injured?'

One of the assembled riggers made space for Stiles next to the perforated aircraft.

'We don't know, sir,' he said. 'He's not responding to anything we say.'

Stiles climbed onto the wing root, crouching to put his face level with Morris' head. The other man was staring ahead, only his eyelids fluttered and his lips moved slightly as he spoke to himself.

'Morris?' Stiles leaned closer. 'Are you hit?'

'...as we forgive those who trespass against us. And lead us not into temptation...'

'Morris?'

'...but deliver us from evil. For thine is the kingdom, the power and the...'

Stiles grasped the other man's shoulder.

'…glory-' Morris snapped his head around, locking eyes with his flight commander.

Stiles softened his face into a smile.

'Are you hurt, son?' he asked. 'Where are you hit?'

Morris looked down at his body, as if its presence beneath his face was a surprise.

'I don't think I *am* hurt, sir' he replied.

Stiles glanced at the shattered instrument panel in disbelief.

'Well' – Stiles squeezed the other's shoulder in encouragement – 'let's see if you can stand up.'

Morris stared back into his eyes, frowning slightly as he digested the suggestion, then nodded.

'Yes, sir,' he said.

Bracing on the mangled rim of his cockpit, he hauled himself to his feet. Stiles took his hand and helped him onto the wing and down to the grass.

Two men jogged up with a stretcher, placed it on the ground and looked at Morris expectantly. Morris smiled sweetly at them.

'There's no need,' he said. 'I'm perfectly well, thank you.'

'We'll let the medical officer give you a look over anyway.' Stiles placed a supportive hand on the dazed pilot's back and they walked off towards the medical hut, the unladen stretcher bearers trailing in their wake.

The rigger watched them move away, then returned to assessing the damaged biplane.

'Well, I'll be…'

The soft exclamation drew the man's curiosity and he looked up to where an armourer was examining the Pup's machine gun.

'Well, you'll be what?' he asked.

The armourer grimaced around his cigarette. 'He hasn't fired a single bloody bullet.'

***

The sky darkened; dove-grey degraded to a dappled ash that decayed to solid ebony as the light was slowly sucked away. Benn watched its progress from the mess window, welcoming the night's benign embrace that buffered him from the malevolence of tomorrow's patrol.

'Where's Morris?' he asked.

'He's in his bunk, sparked out,' Platt answered from across the room.

'Sleeping as soundly as the Frenchman,' Potter leered at his own joke.

63

'Let the Frenchman lie,' Minton's voice was low but rippled with authority. 'And Morris deserves whatever luck he can get. We all do.'

'Luck?' Benn turned to face into the room. 'Morris and his engine were the only two things on that Pup that weren't shot to hell. The bloody thing broke in two when they tried to haul it off the landing strip.'

'He has angels on his shoulders,' Platt murmured.

Benn darted his gaze at the other man. 'What do you mean, angels?'

'He was destined to become a priest, or so he told us,' Platt said. 'He only joined up because some daft tart pinned him with a white feather.'

'He's a bloody liability,' Potter's tone was hard. 'He said outright that he won't be firing his gun. Out of love for his fellow man or respect for creation or some such drivel. With all due respect to God, even I understand we have to kill off the Germans before we can start thinking about peace and harmony.'

A smile crept across Benn's features. 'If everyone thought the same way as Morris, we'd already have peace and harmony.'

'Don't be such a prig.' Potter shook his head in disgust. 'Morris would see me shot down in flames rather than shoot a Hun off my tail. Where's the love for his fellow man when I need some of it.'

'Revolutions only need one seed,' Benn mused.

'I'm not a philosopher, nor am I a poet,' Potter said. 'I'm just an ordinary bloke trying his best to be a soldier. Morris is a mummy's boy and a coward. He's a waste of space, he's a liability and he's in *my* flight.'

'Calm down, lads.' Minton stood and walked to the coat rack, reaching into the pocket of his greatcoat. 'Let's have no more talk of revolution; that kind of talking can put you in front of the firing squad. Here, look what the cook liberated from a cart heading up to the front.' He held a bottle of rum over his head. 'Let's drink to angels, God and courage.'

Chapter 8

Thursday, 29 March 1917

Stiles crunched through the frozen grass, leaving a trail of crushed blades in his wake. He followed the track of previous footprints that led from the farmhouse to one of the canvas hangars. He glanced at the concrete sky and wondered for one disconnected moment if his daffodils at home would survive the thumbscrew of a frost that drained the colour from the heavens and the warmth from his blood.

He paused inside the hangar entrance, extending his hands over a brazier and enjoying the woody smell the heat milked from his leather gauntlets. He cast around for the squadron commander and spotted him dressed in white overalls with a paint pot dangling from his grasp. Stiles watched as Claypole added the finishing touches to a white skull-and-crossbones on the Nieuport's black tail. Seemingly satisfied, the major walked around to the other side of the aircraft. Noticing Stiles, he held his gaze for a moment, then bent to resume his painting.

Stiles walked the short distance that separated them.

'Good morning, sir,' he said.

'What do you think?' Claypole nodded at the decoration. 'I got that cook to draw the outlines in chalk. He's a bloody good artist, used to make a living from it apparently. Makes me wonder why he's not a better chef.'

'I was hoping you might change your mind about this flying thing, sir,' Stiles said. 'It can only end in hot water. What if you don't make it back.'

Claypole daubed white paint into the chalked outline.

'Tell them I've deserted,' he said.

'It would make things awfully difficult,' Stiles continued. 'The regulations-'

'If we carry on losing pilots at this rate' – Claypole interrupted – 'Jackdaw will cease to exist before the end of April. I'm not prepared to stand here and watch a new bunch of half-baked clowns turn up and take over a squadron I've worked hard to build. I've already settled matters with one Hun pilot and I intend him to be the first of many.'

Stiles looked down and shuffled his feet.

'As it happens, half-a-dozen replacements have just arrived,' he said. 'Do you want to speak with them?'

'No!' The commander's shout drew furtive glances from riggers working on nearby Pups. 'No.' Claypole's voice dropped to a hiss. 'Not this time. They'll learn what they need in the pilots' mess and in the air. If any of them last more than a week, report their names to me. I'll talk to them then.'

Stiles stared for a moment into the blank eye-socket of the painted skull.

'Yes, sir.'

He turned, walked back to the hangar entrance and paused. Engine noise rolled in towards the field and biplanes emerged from the haze like wraiths summoned to a coven, the roundels on their wings staring like startled birds.

The flight of Pups circled once and dropped into their landing approach. Five had left on the patrol, only four returned. Stiles blinked as the steely cold air gouged a tear from his eye, then set off along the trampled trail, back towards the farmhouse.

***

Benn pushed through the mess door with the two other members of Mumford's patrol. Silence fell over the pilots in the room, punctuated by Minton, tapping out his pipe. Benn shrugged his heavy leather jacket onto the floor and advanced on the silhouette wall.

'Can't we stop playing this bloody awful game?' Morris sprang from his seat in outrage.

'No!' Benn searched through the profiles and pulled Scarlett's head from its place, screwing it up in his palm. 'We're not allowed to stop playing until Beadle blows the final whistle.' He lobbed the ball of paper at Morris. It bounced off the man's chest and dropped to the floor.

'How did he go?' Minton looked up from refilling his pipe.

'In flames,' Benn said. 'Isn't it always in bloody flames? We didn't even see what hit us. We were trundling along looking for our rendezvous and suddenly Scarlett's a flamer and a silver-grey Albatros is diving away and running for home.' Benn paused, shaking his head in short, tight motions at the memory. 'Mumford just kept on going, straight and level. We stayed in formation, as if nothing had happened.' He rounded on Morris. 'That's four out of six of the new boys who have snuffed it in a dozen days.'

'Give it a rest, son.' Minton's tone matched the gravity of his gaze.

Benn looked around the room. Half-a-dozen fresh, pallid faces he didn't recognise looked back at him with fright glittering in their eyes.

Benn's shoulders sagged and he sat in the chair next to Morris.

The other man looked at him and his frown softened with empathy.

'I'm sorry,' Morris said quietly, resuming his seat.

'Don't be.' Benn's chin rested on his chest and he stretched his legs out before him to chase out the cramps of cold. 'It's a bloody numbers game, and Scarlett's number came up.'

Morris nodded silently.

'Except' – Benn swivelled his head – 'your number came up yesterday, but you walked away from it just fine.'

'I was lucky.' Morris squirmed under Benn's subdued hostility.

'Platt thinks that God has given you a guardian angel,' Benn said. 'Maybe God still wants you for a priest.'

'That's not true, I...'

'But apparently, God frowns on you if you defend yourself,' Benn persisted. 'He doesn't want you shooting at anybody.'

Morris swallowed hard, but stayed silent.

'It seems to me that it's God who is playing the games,' Benn said. 'Cruel... terrible... unfair games.'

'Leave him be.' Minton stood and walked to the stove. He opened the door and flipped the smoking logs over. 'Show some respect for the boy's feelings.' The dry wood burst into renewed flames that licked out of the opening and sent smoky tendrils towards the rafters. 'We're all in hell. We should all be able to choose how we get through it.' He clanked the stove door shut.

Benn watched Minton return to his seat. 'Tell that to Scarlett.'

Friday, 30 March 1917

'Fuck this.' Claypole stood up and grabbed his greatcoat.

'Fuck what?' Stiles rocked back on his chair.

'This farmhouse and this bloody airfield,' Claypole said. 'I need a drink. Who's coming?'

Stiles stood up, grinning.

'I've never been one to turn down a wet on a cold and frosty night,' he said.

Mumford smiled apologetically.

'I'm afraid I don't drink, sir.'

Claypole raised an eyebrow and switched his gaze to Hartley, who chewed his lip for a moment and then shook his head.

'I've got two new-boys in my flight for the dawn patrol,' he said. 'I can't afford to be hungover.'

'Right, come on then, Davenport,' Claypole said. 'Get your coat on.'

Davenport stuttered, 'I think I'd rather-'

'Get your coat on, you're coming,' Claypole insisted. 'I can't have the French thinking me and Harry are a couple of old theatricals, can I?'

Davenport stood, glanced regretfully at the roaring stove, and shrugged into his greatcoat.

Claypole led them out into the night. A desultory rain flicked at their faces and beaded onto their heavy woollen coats.

'We'll take that truck.' The Major gestured at the rickety vehicle on the edge of the field.

'Where are we going?' Stiles asked as they strode over the mud-slicked turf.

'West. We'll trundle about until we find something,' Claypole replied.

The three men clambered into the truck, Claypole taking the driver's seat. The engine kicked into life at the third attempt. Claypole rooted in his pocket, pulled out a hiker's compass and threw it into Davenport's lap.

'West,' Claypole repeated and released the handbrake.

The truck bumped over the rough grass, lurched through the gate and roared off down the road. Heading south, Claypole pulled the first right turn he came across. The single windscreen wiper flapped backwards and forwards at a manic pace, but he still had to lean close to the glass to see a way forward.

The road cut its route across flat, featureless fields. The limited dome of illumination from the lights created the illusion that the road was flowing under a stationary vehicle that dangled helplessly in black space.

'Shit, I hate France,' Claypole muttered to himself.

The road passed through a belt of trees, beyond which the way was edged by small dwellings interspersed with barns. The thoroughfare curved into the centre of the village where four roads met, converging on an open square that was dominated by the dark hulk of a gothic brick church. Claypole pulled up in front of the church.

'Where I come from, wherever there's a church, there's generally a pub nearby.'

The three men piled out of the truck into the damp night. Fifty yards down the road, an enamel sign adorned the side of a white-painted, single-storey building. It showed a picture of a cockerel crowing next to a bottle. As they walked towards it, the door opened and the hubbub of conversation spilled into the night.

'Bingo!' Claypole exclaimed.

The group strode to the building and pushed in through the door. The hum of conversation momentarily lulled to silence and then resurged, settling at a quieter level. The pilots found an empty table by the small fireplace, shucked off their coats and sat down. An elderly lady walked over from the counter and stood by the table, an attentive half-smile on her face.

'We need some beer,' Claypole said.

'Bière pour trois s'il vous plait,' Davenport echoed.

The waitress nodded, her smile broadening.

'And some bread and cheese.'

'Et du pain et du fromage. Je vous remercie, Madame.'

The waitress moved away and Claypole swivelled to face Davenport.

'What do you think you're doing?' Claypole asked. 'She's perfectly capable of understanding English.'

'I was just being polite, sir,' Davenport answered. 'It's their country after all.'

'Well, none of this lot look like they're doing very much to save it,' Claypole hissed.

'In all fairness, sir, the southern end of the line is with the French army.'

Claypole snorted. 'And the northern end is with the Canadians.'

The waitress returned and placed three tumblers and a jug of ale on the table.

'That's a bloody long way to come, and none of *them* are French.'

Davenport exchanged a glance with Stiles, but decided to let the argument lapse.

Stiles poured out the beer, pausing to let the foam subside before topping up the glasses.

'They look prettier on the syphilis posters,' he said.

Davenport took his glass. 'Excuse me?'

'The waitresses.' Stiles took a swig of his beer. 'We must be in the wrong pub.'

'Estaminet,' Davenport corrected.

'Excuse me?'

'It's French for tavern.'

Claypole leaned forward: 'Where did you learn to speak French?'

'I went to a boarding school,' Davenport said.

Claypole surveyed the other's face while he sipped his drink.

'You weren't involved in the theatrical society, by any chance?'

Stiles laughed, snorting beer out of his nostrils and, while he choked his airways clear, the waitress returned with a tray.

Claypole's eyes widened as the woman placed a bowl of steaming stew in front of each of them, a large platter of bread and cheese in the centre of the table and a bowl of dried fruits next to it.

'What's all this?' he murmured.

Davenport smiled his thanks to the waitress as she left.

'I suspect it might be an expression of gratitude,' he said.

Silence dropped over the table as the men tore off chunks of bread and dipped them in their broth. The ale jug emptied and another was brought to the table.

Eventually Claypole pushed away his empty bowl and cut off a chunk of cheese. He looked at Davenport, his eyes narrowing.

'Yours is the only flight that hasn't lost anyone in the last two weeks,' he said.

Davenport dabbed his mouth with his napkin and took the statement as a question.

'I have good pilots who look after each other,' he said. 'Lieutenant Minton in particular is like a proud gamekeeper.'

Claypole nodded his understanding as he chewed his cheese.

'And of course, we fly by the rules you've laid out,' Davenport continued. 'Rule one: Stay in formation-'

'Yes, thank you, Davenport' – Claypole cut him short – 'I know the bloody rules.' He reached inside his tunic and pulled out a folded sheet of paper. 'This was circulated from HQ yesterday. It's been handed down from Trenchard himself.'

Stiles picked up the paper and scanned it, mumbling as he read: '...*force the enemy to fight well behind, and not over, the lines...*' – his eyes moved back and forth – '...*offensive patrols, pushed well out to the limits of army reconnaissance areas...*' – he took a draft from his glass – '...*not give way to requests for the close protection of corps machines, except when such machines are working at an abnormal distance over the lines.*' He refolded the order and looked up. 'Well, this flips everything onto its head. Into the lions' den we go.'

Claypole nodded: 'Our battle zone will now extend fifteen miles or more behind the enemy front.' He pulled a wan smile. 'At least Hartley will be pleased. He suggested the very same thing only the other day.'

'It's all very well for Hartley,' Davenport said. 'That's man is like a bloody terrier; he's got killer instincts. But most of our lads are plodders. They'll do a good job when they know the rules, but they're hardly swashbucklers.'

Claypole swilled the remains of his beer around the bottom of the glass.

'It's no more or less dangerous than going over the top,' he said.

'Exactly,' Davenport muttered. That's what worries me.'

Chapter 9

Saturday, 31 March 1917

A savage wind lashed across the meadow. The hangars' canvas walls ballooned and flapped dangerously and hailstones rattled against the windows of the huts arrayed along the edge of the aerodrome. Flint grey clouds pressed low upon the earth, dragging with them long misty fingers that reached down, as if in curiosity, to touch the alien solidity of the soil below.

Platt sat on his cot, his back against the plank wall, a notepad resting on his knees. He wrote carefully in small, looping script, seeking out ways to describe his situation that wouldn't terrify his mother. The hail's muffled clatter vibrated gently against his shoulder blades, a strangely comforting sound that guaranteed the squadron's respite from combat patrols.

The rasp of tearing paper de-railed his concentration. He tutted to himself and paused his writing, doubling back to re-read his last paragraph. Back in the flow, he licked his pencil and set it back on the paper. Another ripping noise knocked him out of step and he glared across the hut at the source.

Benn lounged on his cot with a book held open in front of his face. Platt watched the other man's eyes moving backwards and forwards as he read. Benn licked his finger and flipped the page, scanning it with rapt attention. Then he tore the page from the book and let it drop to the floor where it settled with the previous two on the mud-stained wooden floor.

'What are doing?' Platt asked.

Benn let the book drop to his chest.

'Reading. What does it look like?'

'Why are you destroying the book?' Platt asked. 'Someone could read it after you.'

Benn frowned: 'Why should I give a jot about what happens *after me*?'

'Because it's the decent way to think.'

'Decent?' Benn propped himself up on his elbow and glared across at the other man. 'Is it decent to hide a man's body and steal his aeroplane? Are you writing *that* in your letter to mummy?'

'I didn't have a choice,' Platt said. Captain Stiles could walk away, but I'm just a bloody lieutenant. You know Claypole as well as I do. If I'd refused, he would've made my life hell.'

Benn's gaze stayed level but he said nothing.

'And anyway' – Platt closed his notebook – 'if the Frenchman had died a minute earlier, he would have crashed and burned two miles away and we'd never have seen hide nor hair of him.'

Benn returned to his reading.

'Say what you like about him,' Platt persisted. 'I hear Claypole's already bagged one Albatros using the Nieuport, and who knows, that may save someone's life, perhaps even yours.'

***

Stiles grimaced as another swathe of hailstones slashed across the farmhouse window. 'Bloody weather,' he muttered. 'Now we know what we have to do, I'd really like to be getting on with it.'

Mumford looked up from his newspaper.

'Perhaps the weather is a blessing,' he said. 'At least no-one's getting killed today.'

Stiles nodded: 'None of *us* will be getting killed, that much is true. But someone is being killed somewhere out there, you can be sure of that.'

'What are the pilots doing?' Claypole's question cut across the conversation.

'Exactly what we are, I suspect,' Stiles answered.

'Can't they assemble ammunition belts?' Claypole suggested.

'We've stocked up enough for several patrols,' Stiles said. 'The armourers are a bit twitchy about having them hanging around too long in damp weather.'

'I see,' Claypole said. 'In that case, you and Mumford can take your flights out for a little drive. I found last night's trip to be very therapeutic.'

'In this?' Stiles jerked a thumb at the window.

Claypole regarded him from beneath a frown: 'It's a covered vehicle, isn't it?'

***

The clouds loured with persistent menace, but the hail had passed over by the time the truck mounted the road running past Vert Galant and hauled its way north, away from the farm. Stiles gripped the steering wheel with gloved hands, his forearms vibrating in resonance with the growling engine.

'What is wrong with the man?' Mumford sat in the passenger seat, swaddled in his greatcoat, a fur-lined leather helmet pulled down over his ears.

'The major?' Stiles glanced at the miserable bundle hunched next to him. 'He's a strange bird, I'll admit, but he's doing his best to keep the squadron safe.'

'Safe?' Mumford's voice rose a tone. 'We're within a week of another bloody, meat-grinding disaster, a pointless, self-defeating re-run of the Somme, and he sends us out on a day trip in this clapped-out charabanc as if it's a bank holiday in Clacton.'

'It's not so bad.' Stiles smiled wryly. 'Have you ever been to Clacton?'

The truck bumped on, entered the town of Doullens and shuddered to a halt at a road junction. A soldier stood, palm upturned, halting them in favour of a line of heavy trucks jolting their way east.

Stiles sat drumming his fingers for a few moments as the dark-green vehicles snaked past, then lost his patience, slid down the window and shouted out to the soldier, gesticulating in the direction the column was moving. The soldier nodded and waved them in to join the traffic.

'Ah, that's better,' Stiles sighed to himself, as he settled into the steady pace of the convoy.

Mumford looked warily across the passing landscape, then squinted at the vehicle ahead of them.

'That looks like an ammunition truck,' he said. 'I think we're on the road to Arras.'

'We're on the move,' Stiles replied. 'That's the main thing.'

Ten minutes passed. The monotonous drone of the engine that dragged them east nibbled away at the edge of Mumford's nerves. Then the note dropped an octave as the column slowed to a crawl. The truck in front crabbed across to the right, its tire walls grinding against the verge. Stiles dropped another gear and tucked in behind.

'It's infantry,' Mumford said. 'Poor bastards.'

The tail-end of the marching column came into view as the trucks crawled past it. The men walked out-of-step, which gave their formation a curious undulating gait. Most wore rain-capes that covered their packs, and with helmets tilted forward, they had the air of disconsolate hunchbacks, anonymous in the press of their fellows.

'This won't do,' Stiles muttered. A minute later he lurched the truck off the main road onto a track heading south.

***

The eight pilots huddled on the benches in the back of the truck lurched in sympathy with the hard turn.

'Perhaps they're driving us over the lines to surrender,' Potter smirked. 'It'll be sausages for tea tonight.'

'Mumford might consider that. But it's Captain Stiles who's driving,' Platt answered. 'He's what Davenport would call a Good Egg. I reckon he'll drive us around in circles for an hour or so and then look for a tavern.'

Two of the new replacements sat together at the end of the bench.

'Shouldn't we be flying?' one of them asked and then smiled pleasantly into the faces that turned his way.

Benn shook his head and looked away. Platt pulled the canvas drapes at the back of the truck aside and nodded at the weather.

'Flying in this isn't a problem,' he said. 'It's the not knowing where you are while you're flying, or where to land when you've finished flying that spoils the fun.'

'What did they teach you at flying school?' Benn asked.

'How to fly,' the young pilot said.

Benn nodded sagely and a torpid silence descended over the group, disrupted by the grinding of gears as the truck slowed down to a crawl.

The vehicle whined on in first gear for a while, then clonked to a halt. The slamming of doors reverberated in the cold air and the tailgate dropped, inviting the pilots to exit. The eight men slid along the benches and climbed out onto the frozen earth, tightening mufflers and turning up collars against the cold.

'Where are we, sir?' Potter asked his flight leader.

'Somewhere just behind the last summer's front lines,' Stiles answered. 'I'm not sure where we are exactly, but I thought it might be worth a look.'

The ragged group started down what appeared to be a track where the shell-holes had been filled and some sections strengthened with stretches of mud-stained duckboard. The land to either side was a barren expanse, levelled but not flat. Craters that bisected craters pocked the earth, scars that spoke silent testament to continuous massed-battery barrage. The shattered shafts of carts and the limbers of gun-carriages protruded from the earth like the naked, impotent flag poles of a decimated empire, and empty ammunition boxes rusted their iron-red flakes to colour the nearby mud sienna.

The men walked east, parallel to communication trenches that slashed the soil in languid zig-zags, containing between their sagging walls puddles of indeterminate depth, covered now with ice that gleamed with an oily pearlescence, like the dirty scales of a skulking reptile.

The track petered out and each man picked his way forward across the uneven, slippery ground until they stood along the edge of the frontline trench. Littered with the paraphernalia of soldiery it now stood empty and silent, exuding a faint miasma of faeces. Rusting corned beef cans and crumpled cigarette packets dotted the fire step; a forgotten greatcoat hung from a trench ladder, green with mould, sodden and sagging.

Rusty wire coiled along the edge of what had been no man's land, drops of water coalescing from the damp air onto its still-sharp barbs. Forced into redundancy by the enemy's retreat, the wire had been dissected and peeled away in several places to allow British infantry access to claim the gifted territory.

'What are those?' Morris asked, pointing to the middle distance. 'Are they logs? Bushes?'

'Christ,' Potter muttered. 'They're fucking blokes.'

Once the ghastly fact was realised, the low, tumescent lumps could be recognised as the vestigial shapes of bodies, flattened, blurred and softened by rain and decay. Then, amongst the fetid bundles of blood-blackened fabric, the spiny profile of a protruding rib-cage might be recognised, and the dull gleam of a bony dome could draw the gaze down to the vacant sockets of a broken face.

Platt put a hand on Benn's shoulder and leaned in to whisper in his ear: 'Dumping that Frenchie in the pit doesn't really seem like the crime of the century after all, does it?'

***

The group trailed back in silence across the empty, blasted battlefield, slipping on mud made slick by the onset of a desultory drizzle that wafted in from the east like shimmering veils of remorse. Arriving at the truck, the men climbed in and shimmied along the benches, brushing the beaded moisture from their greatcoats. The engine kicked into life and the vehicle lumbered through a three-point turn and groaned back along the way it had come.

'It's a real shame the army has so many soldiers,' Morris said. 'If they had fewer men, maybe they'd be more careful with them.'

'It's about to happen all over again,' Benn intoned. 'Only this spring it will be different stretch of wire in a different field.'

'Shit,' Potter hissed in annoyance. 'I've got innards on my boots.'

Chapter 10

Sunday, 1 April 1917

Three neat gashes sullied the smooth doped surface of the Pup's starboard wing, torn by dispassionate shards of steel shrapnel flung into the sky from the increasing density of anti-aircraft batteries sequestered behind the new German lines.

'It seems the Hun Archie is getting up bright and early these days.' Hartley pointed to the damage. 'Patch this up. Make sure it's neat.'

'Yes, sir.' The rigger stuck his hand into the rents, fingering the wooden formers inside, checking for structural damage.

Hartley moved to the fuselage, stroking the flat of his hand along its flanks and stooping to reach under its belly, searching for further damage. An engine coughed to life behind him and he turned from his examination.

The silver Nieuport stood facing the breeze with Claypole running it against the chocks to warm up the motor. Hartley couldn't help but admire the lines of the French machine; the Sopwith had a tidy robustness about its demeanour, but the Nieuport sat squat and pugnacious, its narrow lower wing spoke of restraint, its upper wing, set low above the cockpit breathed a desire for speed.

Claypole waved his hands above his head and his groundcrew pulled the impediments from beneath the wheels. Hartley watched the sleek, silver machine slide into motion, speed across the field and rise into the air, a forlorn pang of envy pricking in his throat.

'Sir' – a rigger trotted up to him – 'we need to run a flight-test on Captain Stiles' plane, but we can't find him.'

Hartley glanced over at the groundcrew manhandling the Pup out of the hangar: 'That's alright, I can do it.'

'Right you are, sir.' The rigger turned to walk away.

'Is it armed?' Hartley called after him.

'Yes, sir. It's all ready for the evening patrol.'

'Excellent,' Hartley murmured to himself, pulling his gauntlets out of his greatcoat pocket and striding over to the machine.

As the engineers hauled the Pup head-on to the wind, Hartley vaulted onto the wing and clambered into the cockpit. The engine fired up and roared into life as he squinted at the eastern sky to pinpoint the receding silhouette of the French plane. Waving away the chocks, Hartley bounced across the grass and hauled the scout into the air. He held the airframe straight and level until his speed picked up, then banked east in pursuit of his squadron commander.

Hartley held the Pup at maximum revs. The man he chased was cruising, so the gap closed steadily as they approached the old frontlines. Claypole was flying low and Hartley stayed lower. Ravaged fields and tracks littered with shattered equipment flashed by barely thirty yards below him, but no tree or church spire was left standing high enough to present any danger of collision.

Hartley closed the range to three hundred yards. Rather than slowing down, he zig-zagged his course into a series of lazy banks to maintain the gap. This would present a profile that Claypole could recognise should he spot his pursuer.

Hartley settled into his hypnotic snaking flightpath, keeping a wary eye on his leader whilst watching the landscape unfold beneath him. The vivid scar of the abandoned frontline gave way to the familiar patchwork of hedged farmland. But these fields were far from fecund. The bloating corpses of cattle and sheep defiled the meadows, orchards lay felled, hay barns stood fire-blackened and roofless.

Hartley looked with professional detachment upon the shambles that the retreating German infantry had left in its wake; after all, it made *some* military sense to inconvenience your pursuing enemy as much as possible.

Then, a broken village appeared in front of his aircraft, some of its fire-ravaged dwellings still smouldered wan coils of smoke into the sky. A lone figure stood at the crossroads in the centre of the razed settlement; a pale, upturned face framed in a hooded, black garb; a pitiful echo of the Reaper that had laid claim to this defiled land.

The old woman looked directly at him as he streaked by, her face containing neither bewilderment nor disdain, empathy nor hate; the weight of her hopeless grief crushed all other expression from her features.

Hartley gritted his teeth against a swell of unbidden emotion as he curved his fighter into the return bank of his fishtailing flight path.

Ahead, through the arc of his propeller, he saw the Nieuport lift sharply above the horizon, climbing away from the dun fields. He pulled out of his zig-zag and flew a parallel course on his leader's starboard side, hauling into a consonant climb, as yet unable to discern why Claypole was reacting. A sudden burst of tracers curved towards the Nieuport's nose, and at their source, a grey-painted Albatros coalesced from the grey-washed sky.

Claypole levelled out and flew straight as the tracer squirmed around him and dropped away like dying fire-flies in the frigid air. As the Albatros overflew him, he pulled up into a loop, slamming into a half-roll at the top. The German hauled into a tight starboard bank and the two fighters ran head-on like jousting birds. This time tracer blossomed through both propellers, cross-stitching the narrowing sky until the aircraft flashed past each other with sparse feet sparing a collision.

Hartley glanced down; the ground was sickeningly close for combat manoeuvres. He eased his nose up and returned his gaze to the fight.

The Albatros banked around to starboard. Claypole kicked into a tight turn to port, teetered on, but avoided a stall, and levelled out to open fire as his committed opponent flew through his bullet-stream. The grey German scout wallowed in the shock of the impacts and made no further attempt to evade the Pup as Claypole dropped squarely onto its tail and poured more fire into the body of the enemy plane.

The Albatros dipped into a shallow dive, flattening out as it approached the ground. The undercarriage struck a low wall, cartwheeling the aircraft, tail over nose, to pancake on the grass of the empty meadow beyond.

Claypole circled once and went down to land on a diagonal track within the walled pasture. Hartley followed him in, touching down and running slightly past his leader's stationary plane. Hartley climbed out of his Pup to find the squadron commander waiting for him, hands on hips.

'Why are you following me around, Captain Hartley?' he scolded.

'Flight testing,' Hartley nodded at his aircraft.

'This is still technically enemy territory,' Claypole said. 'I could put you on a charge for reckless behaviour.'

Claypole turned and strode towards the downed German machine. Hartley followed him.

'That was some very sweet flying, sir,' Hartley said. 'I didn't expect you to nail him so quickly.'

'He banked right twice,' Claypole said. 'It's not hard to shoot down a man who insists on flying in circles.'

They reached the wrecked Albatros, its hot engine hissing quietly against the damp grass. Painted on the grey fuselage, slightly aft of the empty cockpit, and in front of the large black Maltese cross, there was a stylised canine face staring balefully with red, diamond-shaped eyes. Beneath it, in gothic script, was the word '*Silberfuchs*'.

Claypole pulled a lock-knife out of his pocket and sawed around the mascot, tearing the stiff, doped canvas away from the fuselage and rolling it up against his thigh. He cast his eyes around the field.

'Ah. There he is.'

Fifteen yards away from the wreck, the German pilot lay where he had been thrown. The two British airmen walked over to the body and Hartley crouched down to pull off the man's flying helmet. The short-cropped, prematurely grey hair bristled on top of a severely handsome face. A thin trickle of blood escaped the corner of the man's mouth and Hartley's touch roused him enough to draw out a low groan of pain.

'Stand away!' Claypole barked.

Hartley stumbled backwards as Claypole reached inside his flying jacket, pulled out his service revolver and loosed a shot into the base of the prone man's throat. The body jerked at the impact and settled back to stillness.

Distant shouts drifted on the breeze.

'Best be off' – Claypole grimaced – 'it looks like we've stirred up some trouble.'

Both men dashed to their aircraft and clambered in. Gunning the idling engines, they hauled the machines off the rough grass and into the air.

As they climbed away, they overflew the German infantry running across the field towards them. Rifles cracked and bullets ripped the air between the biplanes. Claypole banked away to the west, jinking as he fled.

As Hartley watched him turn, the memory of the forlorn old woman in her shattered village jostled in his head with the image of the clean-cut and well-fed German pilot they'd just left on the ground. He flew on straight, unheeding of direction, intent on simply gaining altitude. When he'd climbed to about three hundred feet, he pulled the stick back and kicked the rudder. The Pup stalled and fell sideways, turning as it fell into a shallow dive back towards the infantrymen who were now congregated around the wrecked Albatros and its dead pilot.

Hartley snarled under his breath as he pulled the trigger and watched his gun draw graceful loops and slashing lines of bullet strikes amongst and around the soldiers. Three men bucked and fell under impacts, the others sprawled and dived for cover. Hartley's Pup swooped over them, like the wings of atonement, and climbed away from the field, chasing the wake of Claypole's silver Nieuport.

***

Hartley landed at Vert Galant and taxied up to the canvas hangar. He climbed out of the Pup to be met by the rigger. Relief softened the begrimed lines of his face.

'Thank heavens, sir,' he gushed. 'I was scared the old girl had let you down.'

'She flew beautifully.' Hartley pulled off his gauntlets and walked away. 'But you'll need to rearm the gun before Captain Stiles takes her up this evening,' he called back over his shoulder.

Across the field, Claypole stood watching as labouring groundcrew dragged the Nieuport back into its hiding place deep in the hangar. Hartley arrived at his shoulder and followed his gaze.

Claypole threw him a sideways look.

'Alright, let's hear it,' he said.

'Hear what, sir?' Hartley asked.

'Your outrage at what I just did to a helpless man.'

'As I understand it, sir' – Hartley's tone was measured – 'what you did fits right in with Major Trenchard's written order.'

Claypole narrowed his eyes and studied Hartley's face, probing the veracity of the man's words.

'In fact,' Hartley continued, 'I'd be honoured to fly freelance with you again, should the opportunity ever arise.'

***

The evening light was fading fast as Stiles trailed back across the field. He stomped into the farmhouse, sat on the bench by the wall and began stripping off his layers of flying gear.

'Any business, Harry?' Claypole asked.

'We saw a flight of three,' Stiles answered, pulling the stocking from his face. 'They kept approaching and breaking off, drawing us further and further east. It was obviously a trap, so I called it off and came home.'

'You've read the General Order, Harry,' Claypole said. 'If we see them, we're obliged to chase them.'

Stiles padded across the floor to the stove in his socks, picked up the coffee pot and cast around for a mug.

'There's nothing in those orders that convinces me I should commit suicide in some cocky Hun's rat-trap,' he said. 'I brought four good men back who'll be better used, when the offensive kicks off, helping our lads on the ground.' He dredged a tin mug from the cluttered sink, poured himself a slug of the steaming black liquid and set the pot back on the stove. 'Now' – he pointed above the door – 'what the bloody hell is that?'

There, nailed to the crumbling plaster, hung the silver fox head, its dull red eyes gleaming through the dope with sullen malevolence.

'It's what's left of one of your cocky Huns.' Claypole looked up at his trophy with a feline smile. 'I'm afraid he met the gamekeeper today.'

Hartley snorted a laugh.

Stiles looked from Hartley to Claypole and back up to the ruby-eyed canine face on the wall. He sat down at the table and pulled out his handkerchief to wipe the grease from his face.

'You probably don't remember how it was before flying machines,' Stiles mused. 'You're both too young. But I can remember when I first saw one of the marvellous contraptions. All wires and struts, it was, like the skeleton of some magical sea creature drifting through the air. I suppose I was about ten years old, and I think I nearly wet myself with the sheer excitement of the moment. I could *not* have been more amazed at how wonderful the world could be. Men sitting in machines that actually flew. Machines that they could steer through the sky; machines that could take them wherever they desired to go. How *utterly* magnificent.'

He took a swig of his coffee and pursed his lips.

'Now, just look at what we're doing to each other with the bloody frightful things.'

Chapter 11

Monday, 2 April 1917 – Arras

Percy stamped his feet on the cobbles, partly to dislodge the dried mud caked on his boots, partly to encourage some circulation to his freezing toes. The sound reverberated around the buildings in the square. Charlie stood with him, leaning against the cottage wall and gazing upwards into a sky that was just beginning its descent towards dusk.

'Rations are late again,' Percy mumbled, lighting a cigarette and flipping the still burning match in a smoky arc through the air. 'This is no way to run a war, I can tell you that.'

A buzz of engine noise caught his attention and he followed Charlie's eyes into the sky. A British bi-plane bored its way across the city, running due west for home. Muzzle flashes sparkled from its gunner, streaming tracer back past the aircraft's tail.

Percy shifted his gaze and picked up two brightly painted German fighters in pursuit, jinking defensively as they closed in on their target. Another glitter of fire bristled from the British rear gunner, then sparkles of return fire lanced from the noses of both assailants. Splinters spun from the hunted plane as bullets stitched along the fuselage, around and through the gunner's position. One of the pursuing fighters side-slipped as it drew closer, unleashing a longer burst of fire from below. Flames erupted from behind the engine and streamed along the fuselage, garish against the gloaming grey clouds, and the biplane arced away like a comet, dropping out of sight beyond the rooftops.

'Strewth,' Percy said. 'That's a hell of a way to...'

He stopped, glancing at Charlie's drawn face, still upturned, watching the victors bank away for home.

'Outnumbered,' Percy started over, looking down at his boots and scuffing a lump of mud off the toe of one with the heel of the other. 'If you're outnumbered, I suppose your number is more likely to come up.' He play-punched Charlie on the shoulder. 'I still think you should volunteer, though,' he continued. 'You know what I mean. Girlfriend? Apple blossom?'

A smile softened Charlie's face and he turned to answer his friend.

'Maybe,' he said. 'When we've finished this labour detail and get to go to the rear-'

'Shush!' Percy held up his hand. 'Listen!'

A deep-throated roar echoed into the square from along the road. It coughed into crescendos – a powerful engine having its throttle cranked – then dropped to a concerted bellow, underpinned by a metallic clanking, like the rhythmic beating of swords upon shields.

'What is it, Percy?' Charlie hissed. 'Are we being attacked?'

'No.' Percy's eyes darted as he tilted his head to locate the noise. 'It's coming from behind us. It's coming from *our* side.'

The noise marched closer, drawing men out their billets, many clutching rifles. The other three emerged from the cottage door next to Charlie. Percy shook his head, answering their unarticulated questions.

The cacophony peaked, freed from its confining canyon of buildings, the mechanical clamour broke like a wave over the cottages. Accompanying the upswell of noise, a monstrous shape breached the square and scrabbled at the cobbles as it clawed its way forward, snorting gouts of black smoke from its rear.

'Cor,' Percy cooed. 'A bloody tank!'

The bulk of the massive vehicle was sandwiched between two elongated lozenge-shaped slabs, offset so the forward point was raised while the rearward point was at ground level. A linked ribbon of track girdled the outer edge of each slab, their raised ridges scoring at the paving as the machine progressed towards the centre of the square. On the flat surface of each side an armoured projection sat like a parasitical bunker, the stubby barrel of a cannon projecting at its forward end from the centre of a rotatable sleeve. The vehicle's dun-brown paintwork was splattered with mud thrown from its unguarded tracks, but retained much of its factory-fresh sheen.

The machine reached the middle of the square and rocked to a halt. With a final cough, the engine dropped to stillness and the last of the thick exhaust smoke swirled away on the breeze. After a long moment of silence, muffled clangs rung out inside the tank and a trapdoor clanked open in its rear. Men climbed out; men in shirt-sleeves or vests who shone slick with grimy sweat. Each man unfurled through the small exit hole and stretched his limbs into the new luxury of untrammelled space. A fine mist evaporated around their heads as their flushed faces gave up their heat to the hard chill in the air. Kitbags were passed out through the hatch and greatcoats were unrolled and pulled onto now quaking shoulders.

Curiosity drew many soldiers from the square's edge towards the strange machine that had come amongst them. Percy was one of them and Charlie followed behind him. Percy craned his neck at the rear of the machine as another man clambered out of the hull.

'Strewth,' he said. 'How many of you blokes are there in this thing?'

One of the tank-men turned to him, pulling his collar up against the needling cold.

'Eight,' he said.

'Eight?' Percy was incredulous. 'Eight, in there?'

The tank-man wiped the sweat from his forehead with his coat sleeve: 'Two for each gun and four to operate the tank.'

'Blimey.' Percy lit a cigarette and offered one to the tank-man. 'I'm not sure I'd fancy that palaver.'

The man smiled and sucked on his cigarette: 'I'll wager I'm better off in there when the German machine guns start their chattering.'

'Oh, no,' Percy shook his head. 'We're a labour unit, we're just here to hump crates. We only came off the line a few days ago. We're not getting involved in this party.'

A large canvas tote bag was unhitched from the tank's roof and the man moved to assist his colleagues haul a large camouflaged netting over the vehicle.

Percy and Charlie drifted back to where the others leaned on the cottage wall.

'In my father's day' – Trevor squinted his disapproval at the machine – 'war used to be about good men, it used to be about proper soldiery.'

'Ha,' Geordie snorted. 'It stopped being about soldiery the moment we started digging trenches.'

Tuesday, 3 April 1917 – West of Arras

The platoon watched their sergeant walk away towards the queue of trucks jamming the road and the throng of men that milled around them. They swung off their backpacks and sat on their haunches, leaning against the stacks of artillery shells that had already been unloaded. Skirting past the tangle of working men down the edge of the road, a column of soldiers moved east at an easy pace under the weight of full packs. They walked upright with heads held high, but the dangerous uncertainty of the impending offensive was written on their many faces; most were stretched with suppressed anxiety, interspersed with a few that cracked with forced jocularity. But the truth lay undisguised in all their eyes.

Percy balled his hands together over his lips and blew warm breath onto his blue-tinged fingers.

'Canadians,' he said, nodding at the stream of soldiers walking past.

Charlie followed his gaze: 'How far have they come?' he asked.

'Anywhere between four- and seven-thousand miles,' Percy said.

'What?' Charlie was incredulous.

'Well, you see' – Percy lit a cigarette – 'not only is Canada far away, it is also very big.'

Charlie nodded in mute acceptance and returned his gaze to the flow of men.

'What's it like there?' Charlie asked.

'Mostly forests and lakes, I think,' Percy said. 'Bears and wolves, things like that.'

'Crumbs' – Charlie looked at the passing soldiers with a growing respect – 'I'd like to visit a place like that.'

'You concentrate on getting yourself home,' Percy said. 'Canada can wait for later.'

The sergeant emerged from the bustle of unloading trucks and walked back towards them. The platoon rose to their feet, pulling on packs and straightening helmets.

'Listen up,' the sergeant called as he approached. 'They've got enough labour to unload and stack. So, we're to hang around here until they find another job for us.'

The column of passing soldiers reached its end. Behind the column two officers walked, one Canadian, one British. The British officer noticed the idle platoon and diverted across the road.

'Who's in charge? His crisp tone encapsulated his assured authority.

'Sir.' The sergeant snapped to parade-ground attention.

'What are you doing here?' The officer cast an appraising glance across the platoon as he spoke.

'We're assigned as a labour unit, sir.'

'Well, now.' The officer glanced away to the phrenetic activity around the ammunition trucks and back to the sergeant's face. He pursed his lips. 'A labour unit with no work to do is not, in my opinion, a labour unit.' He stepped back, pointing at the receding Canadians. 'Join this column, sergeant. Your men will be better used at the front.'

'By whose orders, sir?' the sergeant asked.

The officer leaned back towards the sergeant, his eyes narrowing.

'Don't be facetious, man,' he hissed. 'Join the column.'

'Yes, sir.'

Under the shouted orders of the sergeant, the platoon formed up and followed him east, snaking in the wake of the Canadians towards the outskirts of the shattered city. The officer followed at their rear.

Percy and Charlie trudged along together. Percy's head sagged and his chin bounced against his greatcoat collar in time with his footsteps.

'Why do I have all the rotten luck?' Percy whined. 'I tell you, if I fell into a barrel of breasts, I'd come out sucking my thumb.'

'It's not just you, is it, Percy,' Charlie said. 'The whole platoon has been sold the same pup.'

Percy turned sharply to admonish his companion, but stayed his words when he saw Charlie's face again upturned. High above, an aircraft circled, like a buzzard over a summer field.

'I don't know much, but I reckon that's a German,' Charlie said. 'And he's been up there a good couple of minutes.'

A raucous screech blazed through the air high over their heads as a volley of shells barrelled westwards towards the roadside they'd left behind. The syncopated spatter of their distant detonations was abruptly engulfed in the monstrous roar of a colossal explosion.

The platoon faltered, their heads turning back towards the cacophony. The blast wave rippled along the road, tugging momentarily at cheeks and flapping trouser-legs.

'They've hit the ammo trucks,' Percy said.

His words were truncated by a second, third and fourth detonation that quaked the earth like the raging blows of a berserker's hammer.

'March on!' The officer's voice tore ragged as he fought to be heard. 'Move along!'

The platoon lumbered into hunched movement as fragments of metal pattered onto the road and pinged off their helmets.

Charlie stole a glance back at the thick column of black smoke that coiled its way thousands of feet into the air.

'That's the thing, Percy.' He clapped his friend on the shoulder. 'You never know what worse luck your bad luck has saved you from.'

The platoon picked its way through the broken city, doggedly tailing the Canadians and finally catching them up as they slowed to a halt. Craning their necks over the heads above them Charlie and Percy could see the commonwealth soldiers filing into a dishevelled industrial building.

'They'll never all fit in there,' Percy said. 'And, to be honest, I'd rather not be standing around in large groups out in the open.' He lit a cigarette and surveyed the sky for circling menace.

But the line continued to move and the building continued to swallow the serpent of soldiers that shuffled into its interior. The officer moved to take his place with the sergeant at the head of the platoon and eventually they moved into the building.

On the far wall was a narrow arch built from blocks of chalk. It let down onto a staircase carved in the bedrock that dropped away below ground level. The chalk blocks looked like the giant teeth of a maw into which the soldiers walked like supplicant sacrifices.

'This is blooming strange,' Percy whispered.

The platoon descended a dozen or more steps into a tunnel hewn from the rock. The temperature dropped by a few degrees and a clinging dampness chilled their cheeks. The walls were washed in the dim light from flickering bulbs that were strung out at wide intervals, and the dull clatter of hob-nails on rock echoed along the arched roof. Occasionally galleries opened up on either side, large chambers full of cigarette smoke and murmuring voices that exhaled the fetid smell of unwashed men into the tunnel as the soldiers passed by.

'What is this place?' Charlie asked as they shuffled along.

'An old quarry,' Percy said. 'At least that's my best guess.'

The column of Canadians turned off from the tunnel into a large chamber, but the British officer led the platoon past this entrance and deeper into the tunnel complex. After a short while he too stepped from the tunnel into a chamber that was more than half-full of British infantry. Lights were strung in zig-zags across the ceiling in more generous number than were afforded in the tunnels, and along one wall several long metal troughs stood underneath grimy taps. The air was tart with the taste of stale tobacco smoke and urine.

'Settle down here,' the officer said. 'Rations will be distributed shortly.' He turned on his heel and left the chamber.

Percy shucked off his pack and lowered himself onto one of the straw-filled sacks on the rock floor.

'Well,' he sighed. 'That was a day and a bloody half.'

PART 2

SPREAD

Chapter 12

Wednesday, 4 April 1917 – Vert Galant

Benn stumbled through the shade-filled no man's land that separates deep sleep from consciousness. Wispy images spiralled across his mind's eye, half-recognised yet stubbornly volatile. Beneath this whirling, ethereal dance of phantoms a steady beat insinuated, faint at first, but building upon itself like a wave in treacle, forcing its influence into his perception. Synchronising with the throbbing expansion of this sound, the wraiths in his mind swirled into solidity, their flashing colours muting to khaki and brown, their fuzzy outlines merging into the fearful shapes of marching boots, rank upon rank, pacing in mechanical unison, pounding their way towards the trenches, carrying their hapless torsos onward into the rapacious ravages of splintering steel and deep-gouging lead; the human wraiths he'd seen on the road, stamping their way eastwards to join the relentless, whirling carnival of death. The wave pulsed higher, and higher, then tipped and broke into diabolical cacophony.

Benn started into wakefulness, choking on a ragged gasp of breath, his spine bending away from his cot in readiness to fight or run. The windows rattled rhythmically behind their sacking curtains and thunder rolled like footfall across the roof. He looked up in alarmed confusion to the unlit lamp, gently swaying on its chain amidst a ghostly haze of dislodged dust.

'The barrage has started.'

Platt's voice cut through Benn's bewilderment and his eyes darted across to the other man. Platt sat on the edge of his straw-filled mattress, solemnly lacing his boots.

'Sounds as if they mean it, too.' He treated Benn to a wan smile. 'Get a move on. It's going to be a busy day.'

Benn wiped a line of drool from his chin.

'Shit,' he muttered under his breath. 'Shit, shit, shit.'

***

Davenport sat stock still. His face creased with repressed tension, like a man waiting for bad news from his doctor.

'Are you eating that?' Hartley pointed his knife at the fried egg that lay coagulating on Davenport's plate.

Davenport glanced down at his breakfast and averted his gaze quickly.

'No. I don't think I would keep it down,' he murmured.

Hartley grabbed the plate and tipped the egg onto his own.

'You're not getting windy, are you?' Hartley said.

Davenport pursed his lips and shook his head with small, tight motions.

'I prefer to call it stage-fright.'

Hartley stabbed at the egg with his knife, twirled a crust of bread into the flowing yolk and bit down into its rich sogginess.

'Wasn't it Napoleon who said that an army marches on its stomach?' he said around his mouthful of food.

'No-one listens to the bloody French.' Claypole interrupted. 'At least not if they're intent on winning a war.' He sat down and dropped a sheet of paper onto the table-top: 'I have our orders.'

Davenport focussed on his leader, grateful for a moment's escape from his pit of brooding. The other flight commanders drifted over to the table and sat down.

Claypole waited until Hartley had finished mopping egg grease from his plate and licking his fingers, then looked around his captains.

'What you can hear outside is the opening barrage of the new spring offensive. I understand, when the main event finally kicks off, they'll deploy the best part of three thousand guns. That's double the weight of fire we had last July, which at least shows that they're *trying* to finish the bloody thing this time around.

'This development will, of course, bring our good friends, *Die Fliegertruppen*, under considerable pressure to spot targets for a counter barrage. So, we need to get up there and dissuade them from doing so. I want two flights airborne at once. One to take the northern sector to Arras and Vimy Ridge, the other to patrol south. Hartley and Davenport will go first. Flip a coin for which sector you take.'

'But the weather is atrocious,' Davenport stuttered. 'It's blowing like a banshee out there.'

Claypole splayed his fingers on the order and slid it across the table towards Davenport.

'There are to be no groundings,' he said. 'It's all here in black and white. If a scout is serviceable, it takes off. No matter what.'

Hartley flipped a shilling and held the covered coin under Davenport's nose.

'Heads or tails?' he demanded.

Davenport leaned back from Hartley's oil-begrimed fingers.

'Heads.'

Hartley lifted his hand to reveal the King's sanguine profile.

Davenport looked the other man in the eye: 'I choose south.'

'Good luck, gentlemen,' Claypole said. 'Entice, engage, destroy. Let's put on a performance worth the admission price.'

Davenport and Hartley moved off to put on their flying kit. Mumford drifted back towards the stove. Stiles stayed at the table, picked up the order and scanned its words.

'Can I assume you'll lay off the freelance flights now the main show has properly started?' he asked.

Claypole plucked the paper from between the other's unresisting fingers.

'No, you can't,' Claypole said. 'I want this war over as much as anyone else.'

'In your standard speech to the new boys you always say that a lone wolf very quickly becomes a dead wolf,' Stiles said. 'It makes no sense-'

'What does make sense' – Claypole cut him short – 'is stock piling ammunition. So, make sure the pilots that aren't flying are in the hangar clipping belts.'

'Yes, sir.' Stiles stood and reached for his greatcoat. He paused as he wrapped his muffler around his neck, head cocked to the roar of the guns that were lobbing uncountable shells towards the German front line.

'It's almost enough to make you feel sorry for the poor bastards,' he mused.

'No.' Claypole shook his head. 'It's not nearly enough for that.'

***

Ten Pups lifted away from the frosted turf of Vert Galant straight into the frigid easterly wind, rocking and dipping in the turbulent air.

Davenport gasped against the chill that insinuated its icy tendrils under his flying kit and prodded his muscles into quaking tremors. He watched Hartley's flight ease up to settle 100 feet above him and veered his own flight across to the right in anticipation of their upcoming southerly turn.

The old front lines rolled by beneath his wings. He gazed down at the spectral mist that pooled in ragged shell-holes and strung itself along the trenches where the empty parapets gave it sanctuary from the wind.

Something bucked against his tail; a transient nudge that fractionally dipped his nose for an instant. Davenport craned his neck around to peer at his rudder, straining against the swaddling grip of his muffler. It came again, like a ghostly hand wobbling his aircraft for a second. He peered down into his cockpit at the rudder bar and then twisted again to look behind. The invisible entity pushed a bolt of air against his face, sinking the rim of his goggles deeper into the soft flesh of his cheeks as it passed.

He peered at the scout formed up off his starboard wing as if the answer to this mystery might be found there The plane bobbed in the blustery airflow and the pilot's attention was fixed on his leader as he worked to maintain his position. Davenport recognised him as Hector, one of the recent arrivals; a steady if unremarkable pilot.

Suddenly, Hector's fuselage concertinaed, ejecting fragments of wood and streamers of canvas into the void. The wings slapped backwards from the shattered spar, catching the crumpled tail section like an insect between clapping palms. The liberated engine curved away ahead of the wreckage, counter-rotating against its own torque. and Hector cartwheeled into space, his arms and legs extended into a rigid star as he spun away towards the ground through a rainbow-flecked mist of vaporising petrol.

'Christ!'

Realisation dawned on Davenport and he shrunk deeper into his cockpit as another volley of artillery shells bored tunnels of vortex through the air around his plane. He flailed his arm in the air to signal the remains of his flight and side-slipped away to the south-east, dropping beneath the latticed parabola of whispering British ordnance.

***

Something snagged on the edge of Hartley's vision and he glanced across to see the tilted wings of Davenport's flight banking away onto their patrol line. Behind them, red and blue roundels flashed on a pair of disembodied wings as they tumbled edge over edge through space. He scanned the sky quickly above and behind in search of any lingering assailant. Finding nothing, he led his flight into a wide left bank to head north-east, gently gaining some altitude in a bid to find less turbulent air.

The terrain ahead bore the glaring striations of new British trench-works; the excavated chalk still glowed an unsullied white against the churned soil. Beyond that, the new German lines lay under a pall of dust and smoke that reverberated and bulged with the flash of fresh explosions, like a monstrous firecracker writhing in its own auto-resurrecting frenzy of continuous self-destruction.

With his eyes resting on the glittering ribbon of violence pulsating behind the enemy wire, he perceived the ghostly grey legacy of shells drawing fleeting tracks along his line of sight. They tore into being just below his aircraft and curved gracefully down to terminate in another vivid flash amongst the mayhem. Mesmerised, for several moments he watched the ceaseless procession of ordnance dive like devilish terns to catch and tear at the corralled shoals of German soldiery, then he tore his gaze away to scan the eastern sky in search of enemy scouts.

***

Captain Stiles fumbled the last cartridge into the belt. He let the belt drop to the table and examined his fingers. The flesh protruding from his fingerless mittens was tinged blue, except where the pressure of pushing frigid metal cylinders home had driven away the blood, leaving his fingertips deathly white. He bunched his hands into fists and thrust them into his greatcoat pockets. The rumble of the barrage palpitated his guts, nagging at his stomach like the acid onset of hunger. He looked around at his pilots. Although their faces were haunted with the burden of constant tension, they were all engrossed in their work, lost for the moment in the repetitive task at hand. Except Benn. He sat with a straight back and a pile of completed belts before him on the table. He met the captain's gaze and held it; his eyes gleaming with a shamanic vacancy.

'Alright, everyone,' Stiles said. 'Finish the belt you're working on and get back to the mess for a warm. We'll be flying as soon as the others get back.'

Extraneous engine noise swelled against the ubiquitous resonance of artillery, drawing the officer's gaze to the hangar entrance. Fitters and riggers closest to the opening stopped work and drifted across to look into the sky. Stiles stood and walked across to join them. A flight of six bi-planes circled the field, bright British roundels gleamed from their clean, light-cream undersides. Each chocolate-coloured fuselage carried a pilot huddled behind a low-slung upper wing and, behind him, a rear-facing gunner. The flight leader peeled off and dropped into a landing approach.

Stiles turned to the nearest mechanic.

'What the hell are they?' he asked.

'Don't know, sir,' the man replied. 'Nice looking aeroplane, though.'

Stiles walked out onto the field, wincing as the wind bit into his cheeks. The other planes descended one-by-one and he kept a wary eye on their track as he crossed the grass to where the leading aircraft had taxied to a halt. He waited at a respectful distance while the pilot shut down his machine. The man clambered out, spotted him and walked across, trailed a yard or two behind by his gunner.

'Captain Mungo.' The pilot proffered his hand. 'We've been assigned to fly from this field for the duration of the offensive.'

Stiles accepted the shake and looked beyond Mungo to his crewman.

'The crew's mess is that wooden building over there,' he called to the gunner, then: 'Come with me, Captain. I'll introduce you to the squadron commander.'

They started towards the farmhouse.

'What's it been like on this sector?' Mungo asked.

'Rather rough, I'm afraid.' Stiles raised his voice against the gusting breeze. Most of the time we're up against the Albatros, so quite often it doesn't end very well.'

'Excellent.' Mungo beamed. 'Just as I'd hoped.'

Stiles shot the man a sideways glance as they ascended the farmhouse steps. He opened the door and ushered his companion into the warm air inside.

Claypole looked up from his paperwork and frowned at the stranger.

'May I introduce Captain Mungo.' Stiles unravelled his scarf. 'This is Major Claypole. He runs the show here at Vert Galant.'

Mungo snapped to attention and threw up a stiff salute. Claypole nodded vaguely in acknowledgement and watched the two men shrug off their greatcoats.

'Captain Mungo's flight is stationed with us while the offensive is on.' Stiles went to the stove and poured two mugs of coffee while Mungo sat down opposite Claypole at the table. 'The captain is very keen to get to grips with an Albatros,' Stiles continued.

Mungo nodded cheerfully as he accepted the coffee and cupped his hands around the mug to warm his fingers.

Claypole leaned forward: 'Why?'

Mungo sipped at the coffee.

'Because our fighters are superior to the Albatros,' he said.

Claypole stood up and walked to the window. He pressed his nose close to the glass and surveyed the new bi-planes lined up in the field across the road.

'What are they?' he asked.

'The Bristol F2.' Mungo blew steam across the rim of his mug. 'It's the future of fighter planes. I think they call it the state of the art.'

Claypole sauntered back to the table and sat down.

'What makes it so special?' he asked.

'It can climb 2,000 feet higher than any Albatros has flown' – Mungo put down his mug and leaned back in his chair – 'and it's ten miles an hour faster.'

'Really.' Claypole glanced at Stiles and back to the newcomer. 'As much as that?'

***

Minton pushed through the door into the pilots' mess. The two other men from his flight straggled in behind him. Benn jumped out of his seat dodging his head around to see their faces as the returning men pulled off their scarves.

'Where's Hector?' he asked.

Minton looked at him, strain and sorrow in his eyes.

'He's not coming back,' he said.

Benn darted across the room to the silhouette wall and plucked Hector's likeness from the shrinking ensemble. He held the scrap of paper in his palm, smoothing out its surface with the fingers of his other hand.

'How did he catch it?' he asked.

Minton pulled a wad of tobacco from his gnarled leather pouch and thumbed it into his pipe.

'His Pup fell apart. Disintegrated.'

Benn gazed at the older man with a quizzical frown.

'One of our shells went through him.' Minton lit a match and sucked its flame into his pipe-bowl. 'There he was, sitting in his cockpit, and the next moment he was spinning in the air.'

A look of amused incredulity infused Benn's features as he absorbed this dramatically novel end. He opened his mouth to ask another question but a sharp gasp of breath distracted him. He turned to see Morris hunched with his face in his hands.

'Of course,' Benn murmured. 'That means you're the *only* one left from the jolly band of heroes who turned up... what was it... three weeks ago?'

Benn scrunched the silhouette in his fist and put it in his pocket.

'Three weeks.' He shook his head sadly and returned to his seat.

***

Davenport stood by his machine and watched Minton and his two companions walk across the grass and enter the mess. The frigid wind that thrummed through the Pup's rigging pulled tears from his eyes and dashed them across his temples. He swallowed hard to control a surge of nausea. Surely Hector was knocked cold by the shell that demolished his aircraft. He couldn't have been conscious to contemplate the fall, to see the rushing ground, to measure his time, to anticipate…

The feral growl of aero engines intruded into his obsessing and he gazed up as Hartley's flight neared the field. Five planes; no loss. Davenport spat the taste of foreboding out of his mouth and started back towards the farmhouse.

***

Candles danced in the draught, and oil-lamps suspended from the rafters spread their soft, scented illumination on the officers gathered at the table. The rumble of artillery punctuated a lull in their conversation.

Claypole recharged their guest's glass, topped up his own and passed the bottle on.

'Cheers.' Mungo sipped the deep-red wine and placed the glass squarely in front of him, swirling it gently from its base.

'Of course, they were supposed to have the F2 operational earlier this year but there have been delays at the factories,' Mungo said.

'Why?' Stiles asked. 'Have they been bombed or something?'

Mungo shook his head: 'No. It was down to industrial action. The workers went on strike.'

'Good Lord,' Stiles hissed. 'For what reason?'

'Higher wages' – Mungo grimaced – 'what else?'

'I hope we're not fighting this war just so the bloody Bolsheviks can get a free ride into Britain.' Stiles drained his wineglass and stared balefully at the flaky crimson dregs in its bottom.

'Ten miles an hour faster, you say?' Hartley changed the subject. 'I suppose ten miles an hour is helpful if you're running away.'

Mungo's eyes narrowed. 'We don't intend to run-'

'What about the guns?' Hartley interrupted him.

'One Vickers, forward-firing, and the gunner has a ring-mounted Lewis.'

Hartley shook his head: 'If it can carry that much weight at that speed, why not ditch the extra man and have two guns firing forward? Just like the

Albatros.' He clapped his hands together. 'Or three… Imagine the glorious mess you could make with three machine guns.'

Mungo regarded Hartley with a level gaze.

'I'm more than happy with the F2 as it stands,' he said. 'I'm sure it will put up a good show.'

'In that case,' Claypole said, 'I'll let your flight take the dawn patrol.' He finished his wine and stood up. 'Goodnight, gentlemen.'

The Same Day – Beneath Arras

A dull, growling rumble undulated around the tunnels and chambers, surging and dwindling like the engines of a steamship in rough seas. Breath and body heat condensed into droplets on the rough-hewn walls, coalescing occasionally into runnels that fed the puddles around the chamber's edge. Fetid exhalations rolled in waves from a nearby latrine and the ever-frigid bedrock leeched warmth from any flesh that rested upon it.

Charlie's mob sat cross-legged on their straw-stuffed sacks playing cards, an empty ration box serving as their table.

'We shouldn't be here,' Percy said. 'Our platoon is a designated labour unit. We've got no business being on no bloody offensive.'

'If we'd stayed where we were, we wouldn't be anywhere,' Trevor said. 'God only knows how many tons of shells went up, and how many good blokes went up with them.'

'He's not wrong, Percy.' Geordie squinted at his cards in the flickering light. 'Listen to that barrage. I reckon we'll have to dig the Germans up so we can shoot them.'

'I was listening to some of the other blokes at the water troughs,' Jack said. 'I heard one lad say there's never been so many cannons all pointing in the same direction. They're catching it good and proper over there.' He nodded sagely. 'Good and bloody proper.'

'Imagine' – Trevor folded his hand and dropped the cards onto the box-lid – 'standing next to an artillery piece, tugging that lanyard every time it's loaded and ready, time after time, from dawn to dusk. Imagine never even catching sight of the men you're fighting. Imagine never knowing how many you'd killed and going to church with no idea what weight you carried on your soul.'

The rumble of the barrage swelled and settled, sending a sonic throb through the arched tunnels.

'It's still an offensive,' Percy said. 'It's still going over the top. No amount of artillery has ever changed that.'

Chapter 13

Thursday, 5 April 1917 – Vert Galant

Claypole swung the door shut and, with Stiles by his side, walked down the steps and away from the farmhouse. The same breeze that tugged at the hems of their greatcoats dragged ribbons of damp grey fog across the field. Intermittently the ribbons wove together, momentarily blanketing the landing strip from view.

'I hope it doesn't get any worse,' Stiles said.

'It doesn't matter if it does,' Claypole said. 'We'll fly, whatever the weather.'

They crossed the road and strode onto the airfield.

'I just had a squint at the latest newspaper,' Claypole said. 'There's a feeling that America will be joining in quite soon.'

'Really?' Stiles asked. 'What's rattled their cage?'

'German submarines apparently. They've taken to skulking around the East Coast ports, sinking anything that crosses their path, and much of that is American-owned shipping.'

'Good Lord.' Stiles shook his head in dismay. 'Still, that's good news for us.'

'Of course it isn't good news.' Claypole shot his companion a sidelong glance. 'Once the Americans get involved, we'll never get them out. They'll demand a hand in running everything for decades to come. It's a European war and Europeans need to get it finished before the bloody Americans get here.'

'European war?' Stiles frowned at his companion. 'Most of the troops in the trenches north of Arras are Canadian.'

Claypole tutted: 'You know what I mean, Harry. Stop being obtuse.'

Engine noise crackled against the background rumble of the barrage and the pair paused to look skywards. Two biplanes curved their way towards the airfield. One staggered and wobbled in its flight, the other shepherded it, flying behind and above its charge.

'Mungo's F2s,' Stiles murmured.

'How many went out?' Claypole asked.

'All six. So, there are four missing,' Stiles answered quietly.

'Oh dear.' Claypole's voice was impassive.

Stiles turned to regard his squadron commander.

'That's eight men, you realise?' he said.

Claypole met the other's gaze for a moment, his eyes hard and steady, then he looked back at the approaching aircraft.

The stricken machine dropped away from its escort and lined up to approach the landing strip, the clatter of its damaged engine rose and fell on the gusts of the vagrant breeze. Shreds of canvas flapped in the airflow, marking battle damage on the port wings and fuselage, and a trail of oily smoke pulsed in thick belches from its elongated exhaust.

The craft lurched lower and the pilot pulled back to keep it level. The fighter wallowed on the edge of a stall and curved down to the grass, landing with a jolt. It ran for a few yards before the left strut of the undercarriage collapsed and the propeller struck the ground, throwing up gouts of soil peppered with wood splinters. The port wing gouged at the turf, dragging against the aircraft's forward inertia and pulling it around in a semi-circle to stand on its nose. The air sizzled briefly as the ruptured tank spilled petrol onto the hot metal of the now silent engine. The pilot and gunner twisted in their cockpits, fumbling for their lap-straps in preternatural silence, panic driving their desperate contortions.

With a brief sucking noise, the petrol flowered into flames, funnelling up and around the vertical fuselage and leaping away from the tail to fly free as brief flares of fire in the wind. The trapped men bucked and flailed for several seconds, then stilled, bending under their own weight towards the ground as the flames smudged away the outline of humanity from their faces.

Riggers loped from the hangar, buckets of sloshing water in each hand. Skidding to a halt as close as the heat allowed them, they splashed the base of the fire and then stood, ineffectual and staring, with nothing more to offer.

'Good God in Heaven…' Stiles muttered, staring at the curling flames as they exhausted the volatile fuel and settled to consuming the doped canvas and wooden lattice that now sagged under the weight of the two blackening bodies.

Claypole laid a hand on the other man's shoulder.

'Harry,' he urged. 'Harry, look at me.'

Stiles blinked and turned to face his commander.

'You need to get your flight ready to go on patrol,' Claypole said. 'There's work to do. We need to get on with it.'

Stiles gazed for a moment at Claypole's face until the words sunk through his shock. He took a deep breath, nodded once and trudged towards the pilots' mess, skirting the men gathered around the burning plane.

Claypole looked up to the grey sky and followed the other F2 as it drifted down towards the field, planted its wheels squarely on the ground and taxied away into the rough grass of Vert Galant's perimeter. He walked over to the aircraft, reaching its side just as the polished wooden propeller jerked to a halt.

In the rear cockpit, the gunner's face was drawn and pale, with eyes fixed on the still-crackling pyre in the centre of the airfield where riggers used brooms and shovels to hook the airmen's corpses and pull them smoking from the wreckage. His features slumped in sickly realisation and the first tremors of shock shivered through his shoulders.

In the front cockpit, the pilot slumped forward, his face cradled in his gauntleted hands.

'Mungo?' Claypole moved closer to the fuselage. 'Captain Mungo, are you hurt?'

The pilot dropped his hands and shook his head.

'What happened to your flight?' Claypole asked.

Mungo continued to stare forwards and the skin on his cheeks tightened with the resonance of recollected fear.

'They dropped on us,' he muttered. 'They simply dropped out of the sky and cut us to pieces. I didn't see them until they were amongst us. They were gone before I could react. It was murder.'

Claypole glanced back at the gunner. The man's eyes were now tightly closed and his face twitched in counterpoint with his trembling body. Claypole returned his attention to the major.

'Listen, Mungo.' Claypole's voice was steady and forthright. 'I don't see that there's much else you can help with here. I'm sending you back to the rear. Go back to the base you flew from yesterday. Hopefully someone there can post you to a new squadron.'

The gunner retched and a gobbet of foamy white vomit dropped onto his chest.

Claypole grimaced: 'Good luck, gentlemen,' he said, turned on his heel and walked back towards the farmhouse.

***

Benn had been drawn to the mess window by the sound of the landing aircraft. His gasp of shock first silenced the murmur of conversation in the room, then the soft, keening wail that pushed past his clenched teeth drew the rest of the men across the mess to stand around him. They stared through the weather-stained glass at the burning aircraft, all of them silent now, like reluctant penitents gazing at the belly of a wicker-man.

Morris elbowed through the press, took in the scene, and gently grasped Benn's arm, pulling him back into the room. Benn moved without resistance, swivelling his head to keep the conflagration in his vision until the bodies of the others blocked the view. Then his face snapped around to regard Morris, his sickly-pale visage heightened the vindication that sparkled in his eyes.

'See?' he hissed. 'See how bloody dangerous it is to bring back petrol?'

Morris eased his charge into an armchair.

'They were clumsy, that's all.' Morris kept his voice low to prevent it from trembling. 'Best not to worry about it.'

The mess door opened and Stiles stepped inside. The cold air he brought with him was laced with the hot scent of burning canvas and scorched hair.

'My pilots, get ready,' he called. 'We take-off in twenty minutes.'

Morris watched his flight leader depart and his face twisted into a grimace.

'That means me,' he said quietly.

Benn reached out suddenly and grabbed his hand.

'Good luck,' he said. His eyes flashed with suppressed dread. 'Don't be clumsy.'

***

At the back end of the mess building, Morris pulled on his flying kit. An alien discomfiture infected his grasp and his fingers fumbled on his buttons and buckles.

Platt and Potter finished dressing and left the mess. As they passed through the door, the group at the window began drifting back to their tables and chairs, but a brooding silence prevailed across the room.

Morris wrapped his muffler around his neck and mouth, and pulled his leather helmet down over his ears. He glanced across at Benn. The young man was staring into unfocussed space, breathing in through his mouth and out through his nose, his lips opening and closing with each cycling breath.

The room's warmth drew out beads of sweat to prickle the skin on Morris' cheeks. He bent to retrieve his gauntlets and made his way to the door.

Outside, the breeze chilled the moisture on his face. He pulled on his thick leather gloves, flexing his fingers deep into their stiff protection. A dozen yards away, Platt and Potter stood with their backs to him, talking to Captain Stiles. The flight commander listened and nodded. As he did so, his gaze drifted towards Morris.

Morris made no move towards the group, instinctively certain their discussion centred on him. His eyes drifted away from the trio and settled on the glowing embers that piled against the F2's naked engine. Outside of the ring of ashes the disembodied remains of the aircraft's light brown wings and scorched tail lay forlorn. A few yards away, two lumpen shapes rested under a canvas tarpaulin. A man holding a rifle stood by them, hunched in his greatcoat, stamping his feet against the cold.

Platt and Potter dispersed towards the Pups lined up on the opposite side of the field and Stiles closed the short distance to Morris.

'Are you set to go?' The captain's features were veiled in his usual Vaseline and silk ensemble. His eyes appeared piggish through the two small holes, but his voice resonated with the easy quality of his genuine concern.

'What did they say about me?' Morris countered.

Stiles put his arm around Morris' shoulders, and with gentle pressure, started him walking towards the waiting aircraft. He, in turn, ignored the other's question.

'We've been given a job to do, Morris' – they trudged slowly across the field – 'and at times it's a shocking, nasty job. But if we do it well… if *you* do it well, there'll be more of our lads in the trenches that will get through this thing alive. You have to weigh everything you do against that.'

They arrived next to Morris' bi-plane and Stiles unhooked his fingers from the other's shoulder.

'The time has passed when we can make choices just for ourselves,' Stiles continued. 'We have to act for the common good.' The flight commander winked through the ragged hole in the stocking. 'We have to do what we're told.'

Stiles started towards his own aircraft and Morris watched him go. The urge to run away trembled through his thighs. But he clambered up onto the Pup's lower wing and hoisted himself into the cockpit.

Across the field, a truck pulled through the gates, a white square on its side quartered by a red cross. It bumped sedately across the rough grass towards the canvas tarpaulin.

Good Friday, 6 April 1917

Morris awoke to the instant and urgent clarity of an impending threat. He stared wide-eyed into the blackness, striving to add solidity to the presence that had awakened him. He started at the rough scratching of a matchbox and shielded his eyes against the effervescent glare of a blossoming match. The flame danced for moment, then settled, its orange glow illuminating Benn's solemn features.

'What are you doing?' Morris hissed, half in relief that he knew the intruder. He squinted at his watch: 'For pity's sake, it's four in the morning.'

'You know how to do funeral rites,' Benn said. 'You have the angels on your shoulders. Platt said so.' He glanced away for a moment, as if collecting his words. 'Platt buried the Frenchman and no words have ever been said over the grave.'

'What?' Morris spluttered. 'No. I never properly learned anything. I had a place reserved, but I never made it to seminary; I never actually attended any lessons.'

The match guttered and the room dropped back to darkness. Another rasp, another flare and Benn's face danced back into view.

'You have the angels. You'll find the words.' Benn took the folded trousers from the foot of the bed and pressed them into Morris's hand. 'Come on.' Benn nodded sombrely to himself. 'The Frenchman needs some words.'

Morris sat up and grabbed a candlestick from a shelf by the bed. Benn took it, transferred the flame from the second dying match to the candle's wick, and stood quietly watching as Morris got dressed.

Minutes later the pair emerged into the metallic pre-dawn frost. The cavernous, clear sky speckled its dark vault with stars, and a cold, full moon draped its ethereal light over the crusted grass.

The two men crunched across the turf to the far end of the field where the target butts still stood. Benn stopped on one side of the filled-in pit.

Morris side-stepped his way around the bare mound to the other side. Looking down he saw a couple of rat burrows angling into the disturbed earth. He extended his foot and pressed them closed with his toe.

Morris looked into Benn's face, a growing swell of concern for the man rising in his chest.

Benn caught his eye.

'Words,' he prompted. 'Say the words.'

Morris swallowed his alarm and cleared his throat.

'My grandmother was no angel,' he began. 'But I remember a little verse she used to recite about those who had recently passed away.'

Benn nodded: 'Go on.'

'May the new road upon which you walk always rise to meet your feet. May the wind that sometimes blows, always be at your back. May the sun that shines fall warm upon your face, and the rains that come, fall soft upon your fields. And until we meet again, may God hold you safely in the hollow of His hand.'

Benn looked at him, expecting more.

Morris bowed his head and clasped his hands in front of him: '*Venit hora eius. Veniet et tua.*'

***

Captain Stiles finished his dinner and pushed away the empty plate. Gouts of sleet lashed against the window panes as if thrown by malevolent demons gathering around the house in the evening's deepening gloom. He glanced around the other faces at the table, mildly shocked at the added age their features carried under the undulating glow of the kerosene lamps. Only Claypole's face remained taut, held firm by some unshakeable internal conviction.

Stiles finished the dregs of his coffee and spoke: 'I've got a bit of a dilemma with a pilot in my flight.'

Claypole looked up from his supper.

'Dilemma? Which pilot?'

Stiles exhaled through his nose and continued: 'Second Lieutenant Morris. He holds to certain doctrines that aren't particularly helpful; Christian values…'

'We're all Christians, we all have values,' Claypole said. 'What's the man's problem?'

'Well' – Stiles shifted his weight in his chair – 'Morris is *very* Christian. He had ambitions for the priesthood before the war, but felt pressurised to join up and do his bit.'

'Laudable on both counts.' Claypole squinted at the other man, struggling to discern the issue.

'He has an objection to killing people,' Stiles said. 'He takes a rather hard-line view of the commandments. He's willing to wear the King's uniform and fly where he's told to fly, but he will not use his gun when he gets there.'

A frown slowly creased Claypole's forehead: 'What if his life depended on it.'

Stiles shook his head: 'According to my other pilots, he's adamant on the issue.'

Claypole's frown deepened: 'But surely ours is the righteous cause, so God will naturally forgive us our transgressions against the commandments.'

'Apparently, Morris is not willing to take that as granted.' Stiles leaned his elbows on the table. 'The question is, what do I *do* about it?'

'He's a conscientious objector,' Mumford offered. 'He should get transferred to non-combat duties.'

'It's probably too late for that,' Davenport said. 'He's got to the frontline without raising any objection. A service tribunal will probably see it as cowardice in the face of the enemy. That's unlikely to end very well.'

'Make him carry on flying.' Hartley's voice held a hard edge. 'If he chooses to go down without a fight, that's his business.'

Mumford swivelled his head to regard Hartley in horror. 'But-'

'Leave it where it lies.' Claypole forestalled Mumford's nascent objection. 'We can't send him away this close to the offensive. It would wreck the squadron's morale. If he makes it through the next week, we can deal with it then.' He reached into a messenger bag by his chair and pulled out a map. 'In the meantime, perhaps he can be persuaded to fire at inanimate objects.' Claypole stood and flattened the map onto the table, pushing plates and mugs aside.

'Tomorrow morning we fly in squadron strength against the German kite balloons in this sector.'

He pointed and the other officers squinted at the area of the map beneath his finger.

Stiles let out a low breath.

'That's five miles or more behind the new German lines,' he said.

Claypole nodded: 'There are too many ammunition convoys on the move to allow their observers to stay in the air; the Hun artillery has already caused a lot of unhelpful damage. So, we have to put out their eyes.

'We can expect large numbers of machine guns and anti-aircraft batteries to be there to meet us. So, to minimise that danger, I've decided to make the run in at low altitude.' He looked from face to face. 'Below fifty feet, full power all the way to the target. Once we get there, we zoom-climb to the attack, bank and dive away. No hanging about; there's bound to be a couple of scouts circling above the balloon emplacements. Get low and come home. This time we're only interested in the balloons.'

'Minimise the danger?' Stiles mused, rubbing his chin. 'Surely it just makes the danger a little bit different.'

Claypole pursed his lips as he rolled up the map: 'It's a good job I like you, Harry,' he said in a low, flat voice.

The other officers moved away from the table to make ready for bed. Stiles remained, regarding his squadron commander squarely.

'Will you be flying, sir?' he asked.

A smile softened Claypole's features.

'What do you think, Harry?' he said. 'What do you think?'

Chapter 14

Saturday, 7 April 1917

The pilots of Jackdaw Squadron stood loosely to attention in the callow light of the cold, grey morning listening to Claypole conclude the instructions for the attack.

'Have I made myself clear?' Claypole's voice rang through the iron air. 'Low and fast all the way there. Simply follow your captain, he has the details of your particular target site. I must stress, speed is of the essence, so when you arrive, attack immediately. Remember, these balloons can be pulled down to the ground in less than a minute. They're deceptively difficult to shoot down, but, once they've been hit enough times, they do burn rather nicely. Good luck to you all. Let's get on with it.'

Fifteen Pups, the squadron's full complement of operational aircraft, stood arrayed across the field with groundcrew ready and waiting to start them up. From the hangar, some men pushed the sleek little Nieuport onto the field, its trim, silver body squeezing the faintest glint from the watery sunlight.

The squadron dispersed towards their planes. Claypole caught up with Hartley and clapped a hand on his shoulder.

'I'll be tagging along with your flight,' Claypole shouted above the ascending rattle of starting engines.

'Very good, sir. Let's give them what for!' Hartley shouted back.

The cacophony rose as more engines spat and crackled into life. Pups milled out onto the field with men at their wingtips guiding the pilots, forming them up in flights behind their leaders.

Hartley climbed into his cockpit and fired up the engine. Blue smoke billowed away in the propwash and the wings waggled in reaction to the engine's pulsing torque. He pulled his lap-strap tight and looked across the field as Mumford's flight straggled into the air and climbed to form up to fly a holding circle. A minute later, Davenport's flight followed.

The groundcrew around Hartley's scout pulled away the chocks and manhandled his wings to point him in the right direction. Hartley taxied forward, waving thanks and farewell to the men who now retreated behind his tail. The silver-bodied Nieuport sidled in from the side and took up position behind his port wings, the other two Pups swaggered into place behind his starboard wings. Hartley, grateful that Claypole had not presumed to lead, waved his arm above his head and surged his machine forward across the grass. The rushing air cushioned beneath the wings, lifted his machine and silenced the rumble and jolt of the wheels. The roar of his engine cocooned him in the familiar sense of deadly power that sparked his blood like no other sensation. Smiling, he led his flight up to join the swirl of circling bi-planes.

Stiles was the last to pull his flight into the air and join the circus over Vert Galant. From the centre of the field below, an orderly held a Very pistol aloft. A spindly column of white smoke climbed into the air and blossomed into a searing white flare that drifted away in the stiff breeze. At this signal, each of Jackdaw Squadron's four flights set course for their targets, diving down onto their bearings like ribbons swooping from the top of a maypole.

Hartley led his flight down, flattening out low above the rushing fields and accelerating eastwards. He snatched a look over his right shoulder to see the two other Pups echeloned behind and slightly above him. He glanced to his left.

'God damn him!' he muttered under his breath.

Claypole's Nieuport was tucked in a full ten feet below Hartley's lower wing. Hartley clenched his jaw and eased his bi-plane down to match his squadron commander's altitude. The proximity of the careening earth shot tingles of visceral protest through his loins and the vibrations from the hammering engine seeped a grinding ache into his wrist bones as his grip on the column tightened. The dried-up scars of the abandoned German line flashed by shockingly close, a muddle of scattered planking and rusting wire piled back upon itself. A small party of British troops, busy scavenging materials, crouched in instinctive alarm at the biplanes' approaching roar, their anonymous upturned faces blinking away like pale spectres under the rushing of canvas wings.

Ten miles to the new frontline, five more beyond that to reach the target. Hartley swallowed against a dry throat and fought to ignore the stiffening of the muscles in his arms and thighs.

A long line of newly-dug emplacements draped in netting belched intermittent white blotches from the nesting barrels of British guns. A nervous artilleryman sprawled into the mud, spilling the shell from his grasp, as Hartley's flight banged through the air above his howitzer. Rib-punching concussions chased the biplanes as the web of emplacements flung shells up and over them, far fleeter in their wingless, air-drilling parabolas, destined to blindly meet their mutual enemy in seconds rather minutes.

The road from Bapaume to Arras, roman-straight in the churned and desecrated landscape, rolled into view, empty of traffic. A couple of miles beyond it the German lines lay under the smoke and flash of the British barrage.

Every fibre of Hartley's body implored him to stop this headlong madness and climb, pull his machine away from hard and dangerous earth. He gritted his teeth against the urge, growling through his clenched jaw to suppress the bunching tension in his chest as the terrain streaked by beneath his wheels.

British trenches; wire; a flash of desolate no man's land and the little formation plunged in amongst the exploding shells. Hartley's fuselage jolted sideways from a shockwave on his starboard side and something zinged through the air in front of his face. He looked back over his right shoulder to see the wreckage of a Pup, dismantled by the blast, flop to the ground behind the German trenches. He wrenched his head back around, willing his plane to haul him through the hellfire.

The curtain of smoke parted, helmeted heads bobbed in communication trenches and the crackling pop of rifle fire rippled through the engine noise. Holes in his wing popped noiselessly into being and Hartley clenched his buttocks against the implication.

The ground rose, and the three remaining fighters eased up in unison to follow it. The movement brought a tingle of relief into Hartley's arms and he arched his back to help the tension drain away. Cresting the ridge, the biplanes flattened their trajectory, skipping over artillery emplacements that pointed in the opposite direction.

Ahead, about a mile distant, a small blob hung in silhouette against the grey cloud banks that stacked the eastern horizon. A thrill of triumph prickled across Hartley's skin, dispelling all other emotions, and he pointed his aircraft's nose at the target, pulling his biplane into a shallow climb. Claypole's Nieuport drew level and matched his attitude, and a quick glance behind showed the other Pup was still there, lagging slightly. The flight bored on across the incongruously serene plateau, lifting graceful wings ever higher in a headlong charge towards their floating quarry.

With astonishing suddenness, the air sparked to life with tracers, spiralling up in undulating threads from a dozen points around the balloon station, the glittering harbingers of the invisible hail of machine gun fire that studded their path. At the same moment, the bulbous brown balloon bobbed and shuddered as its mooring lines tightened and tugged at its flaccid, undulating skin.

High above, unobserved, a circling Albatros curled into a stoop.

Hartley noticed that the basket, suspended on cables forty-feet below the balloon's corpulent underbelly, tipped and swung wildly. An object dropped from the basket's edge, its fall arrested by a rapidly billowing parachute.

Hartley kicked his Pup into a sharp side-slip to wrench his gun down to bear on the dangling observer. Claypole soared over him and Hartley heard the Nieuport open up on the balloon a second before he pulled his own trigger. The German soldier danced and jerked for a moment under the impact of the ordnance, then hung limp in his harness.

The space above Hartley erupted in lurid orange light as the balloon blossomed in burning capitulation to Claypole's hammering assault. Hartley banked hard right to avoid the parachute, then hard left to skirt the roiling fabric furnace that tumbled back towards the balloon's winch.

Ground fire had stopped and, as Hartley pulled around in a wide turn, he saw the reason why – the Albatros was busy stitching lines along the length of the straggling Pup as it tried to flee to the west. As Hartley banked towards the battling pair, flames erupted from the British fighter. The Pup's wings waggled in resonance with its pilot's death throes, then it settled into a shallow descent as the fire encased its entire fuselage.

Claypole's Nieuport sank like an assassin from its superior altitude and dropped in behind the Albatros. Catching it as it banked away from its kill, Claypole's long burst of fire peppered the engine and cockpit. The German biplane wallowed onto its back and the dead pilot slipped away from his aircraft to cartwheel, unheeding, into the ground.

Fresh tracer fire flared from a few of the defending gunners as Claypole climbed away to the west. Hartley watched the other Pup plough into a copse of straggly trees, spewing burning fuel through the tangled undergrowth, then chased after his squadron commander, climbing hard as if his very soul was searching for a heavenly sanctuary.

***

Claypole and Hartley walked back towards the farmhouse, leaving ashen-faced riggers counting the holes and rents in their aircraft. Behind them, returning members of Jackdaw Squadron drifted into view, their engines spluttering as they flattened out to land.

'That was a bit prickly,' Hartley broke the silence. 'Not something I'd want to do every day.'

Claypole glanced sideways at his companion.

'Well, let's hope we did enough today, so we don't have to do it again tomorrow.'

They mounted the steps and Claypole paused to gaze back at the airfield. All the circling aircraft had landed and the flight captains were trudging towards the farmhouse. Resisting a primal urge to count the diminished machines, he followed Hartley through the door.

The men threw off their heavy flying kit. Claypole retrieved a notepad and pencil from a shelf and sat at the table. Hartley set a pot of coffee on the stove and stoked the fire's glowing embers into flame.

The three other flight leaders shambled through door in silence, avoiding eye contact like embarrassed conscripts at a VD clinic.

'It's good to see you all safe, gentlemen,' Claypole greeted them. 'As soon as you're ready, I'd like to hear your reports. It would be nice to send something optimistic back to Beadle in double-quick time.'

The new arrivals nodded mutely, shucked off their gear and ambled to the table.

Claypole licked the end of his pencil: 'Who's first?'

Mumford took a step forward.

'It seems we achieved complete surprise. Each of us lined up and put in a good, long burst. Between us, we managed to set the bloody thing alight. But once they'd woken up, the ground fire was intense. Sadly, we lost Lieutenant Higgins. I'm not sure if he was hit or his controls were damaged, but he kept flying east after his attack.' Mumford shrugged in sheepish apology. 'We didn't hang around to see what happened to him.'

Claypole nodded. 'Davenport?'

'Not so lucky for us, sir,' Davenport began. 'I suspect the balloon crew got a heads-up telephone call from one of the Hun batteries we overflew. In any event they'd hauled the thing more than halfway down by the time we got there. So, we stayed very low and shot up what we could. I'm fairly sure we did some serious damage to the balloon and might have caused a few casualties on the ground. But, Lieutenant Munnings' – he blinked at the memory – 'didn't pull out. He went straight into the trees behind the emplacement.'

Claypole scrawled the name 'Munnings' under 'Higgins' in the margin of his notepad. He glanced up at Hartley with eyebrows arched.

'Yes' – Hartley cleared his throat – 'we also found the run in unusually hot. Lieutenant Cobbit flew through an artillery blast as we crossed the German line. It took him to pieces. He had no chance.' Hartley's eyes were drawn to the pencil scratching the name in the notebook. He cleared his throat again. 'We arrived at the target before the balloon crew had taken any evasive action. We were fortunate enough to have Major Claypole flying with us. It was he who set the balloon on fire, and I was able to shoot the observer as he descended by parachute.'

'You were able to *what*?' Stiles stopped wiping the Vaseline from his face and stared at Hartley. 'You shot a helpless man? Doesn't abandoning ship count as surrendering?'

'Harry!' Claypole held up a hand to silence the other officer. 'I imagine if he'd promised to go home as soon as he landed, that might arguably be the case. As it was, he would've been up in the next available balloon causing the exact same mischief.' He nodded at Hartley. 'Continue.'

'Yes, sir. On the way out from the target, Lieutenant Harkin was jumped by a German scout. It was again, the major who was in a position to engage and destroy the attacker. Unfortunately, Harkin was already going down in flames.' Hartley closed his eyes but the scratching of the pencil point teased its way into his ears.

'Harry? What about you?' Claypole said.

Stiles wiped a sleeve across his mouth to shift the last of the Vaseline from his lips.

'We had an easy run in, but there was pretty intense groundfire all around the target. Both I and Lieutenant Potter got good hits on the balloon, but it was Lieutenant Platt who finally set it ablaze.'

Claypole looked up, clasping his hands under his chin.

'What about your priest-boy?' he asked. 'What's his name? Did he attack the balloon?'

'Second Lieutenant Morris.' Stiles shook his head. 'No, he circled the target while we attacked it. He drew the largest quantity of fire, which made it easier for us. Honestly, I've just looked over his aircraft; it's an absolute bloody colander. How he survived I'll never-'

'His gun,' Claypole interrupted. 'Did he fire his gun?'

'No, sir,' Stiles answered quietly. 'It appears he did not.'

Claypole glared at the scribblings on his notepad for a moment, clenching and relaxing his jaw.

'Right!' He looked up at his officers. 'We need to get all the aircraft checked over and patched up, pronto. Meanwhile, I'll get this report back to staff and request further orders.'

'Further orders?' Stiles pointed at the notepad. 'We lost one quarter of our planes today, along with their pilots. Three more days like this and Jackdaw Squadron will cease to exist.'

'In three days, Harry' – Claypole rose slowly to his feet as he spoke – 'the offensive will be over, the German line will be broken, and British cavalry will be riding towards Berlin. Jackdaw Squadron won't need to exist.'

***

In the pilots' mess, the air was caged in a wary silence. The room was bigger, with more empty chairs. Morris sat slumped in one of the chairs. His face and shoulders sagged like a father who had just buried his own children. Benn stood in the centre of the hut, his discarded flying kit lying around his feet, gazing at Morris.

'Admit it,' he demanded. 'Tell us how to do it. Tell us how to find the angels, how to get them working for us.' He pushed his fingers through the greasy locks of his unkempt hair. 'Higgins didn't have the angels. Higgins just kept on flying – flying in the wrong direction.' He paused, took his hand from his hair and stared at his fingers. 'Higgins!' he hissed under his breath and spun on his heel towards the silhouette wall.

Minton stood in front of the paper cut-outs watching Benn. The steel in his eyes stopped the other man in his tracks. Minton held him motionless for long seconds with this implicit threat, then he turned and plucked the remaining portraits from the wall one by one.

Benn burst into enraged motion, running up against Minton's back, flailing his arms in an attempt to halt the desecration.

'What are doing?' he cried. 'Stop it!'

Minton pulled the last face from the wall, wadded the scraps of paper together and tore them in half twice, letting the fragments flutter to the floor.

'Enough!' Minton's voice was firm but calm. 'It's a pointless game. I think we've all had enough of it.'

Minton moved away to a table by the stove and pulled his tobacco pouch from his pocket. Benn crouched to the floor, gathering up the shredded silhouettes.

'It's not fair,' he said in a quiet voice. 'I want an angel.'

Minton struck a match and sucked the orange flame into his tobacco-stuffed pipe bowl.

'All in good time, son,' he said through the silver-grey smoke. 'All in good time.'

Easter Sunday, 8 April 1917

The two officers crossed the road from the farmhouse to the airfield, crunching their way across the frosted grass.

'You *do* know how far it is from Arras to Berlin, I take it,' Stiles said through a smirk. 'I pity the cavalry their sore arses after that particular ride.'

Claypole shot him a sideways glance: 'You know exactly what I meant, Harry,' he countered. 'Stop being so bloody obtuse.'

'In all seriousness, though, we *will* need more pilots and planes very soon,' Stiles said.

'We'll have to carry on with what we have for now,' Claypole said. 'We're unlikely to get anything through, what with the big show about to kick off.'

'Do we know when they're blowing the whistle, exactly?' Stiles asked.

'It was supposed to be today' – Claypole shook his head – 'but someone has cocked something up along the line. Which is why we've been lumbered with church services to fill the gap.'

A khaki motorbike gunned down the road and turned onto the field. A wooden box suspended on a shoulder-strap sat across the rider's back, and his greatcoat flapped open to reveal his vestments underneath. The rider bumped his way past the officers, waving as he went, and headed towards the main hangar. The two walking men trudged along after him, following the wobbly lines the tyres left in the frost.

'So, tomorrow?' Stiles asked.

Claypole glanced at his companion, his eyes flashing over a wry smile: 'You could probably bet your life on it, Harry.'

They reached the hangar and entered the cavernous space. The pilots and groundcrew stood in loose ranks in front of a trestle-table. The priest had thrown a grubby white cloth over the table and had placed a small brass cross in its centre flanked by two brass candlesticks. He busied himself for a moment lighting the candles.

The other officers stood to one side of the main group. Claypole and Stiles moved to join them, their movements restrained and respectful, infected by the repressive illusion of church that the motorcycle priest had unpacked from his box.

The priest handed a sheaf of song sheets to one of the men and waited in contemplative silence until they had been distributed through the congregation. Once this was done, the priest took a small step forward and raised his chin. His face lit up with beatific joy, as if he'd flipped an internal switch.

'Please, sing with me, *Jesu lover of my soul.*'

The words, flung out from the assembled throats with varying degrees of enthusiasm, were flattened by the dampening acoustics of the canvas hangar. But each line heightened the joy on the priest's face and he was moved to weave the occasional descant through the droning backdrop.

At the end of the hymn, the priest allowed a few moments for the foot-shuffling and throat-clearing to subside, in which time he swept his gaze over his congregation, seeking individual eye-contact wherever possible, before clearing his own throat and launching into the sermon.

'We are here together on this most holy of days to offer our humble worship to the greater glory of God' – he glanced around the hangar – 'in more spartan circumstances and more trying times than we might desire.' He swept the faces again, this time connecting with a few more eyes.

'I suspect you may have found it difficult in your current circumstance to keep a tight grasp on your faith. You may feel that you have earned the right to question how He can be the God of beauty when all around us we see nothing but the ugliness of war. It is perhaps understandable for you to doubt that He is the God of tenderness when we have all witnessed such manifold cruelties. You might be forgiven for wondering what has become of the God of life in the midst of so much death and destruction.

'Today, we celebrate our third Easter Sunday under the heavy yoke of war, hauling together under that yoke the miserable weight of our suffering and deprivation in this foreign land of mud and metal. Yet we *can* find the strength to bear this weight with renewed fortitude, just as Jesus bore the cruel weight of the wooden cross on his journey to the hill where he was to die in suffering to secure the redemption of the world.

'At home, at this very hour, across the sea, those you love, and who love you, will be singing God's praise in churches and chapels the length and breadth of our island nation. It is for *them* that we endure, it is for *them* that we soldier on. It is for *their* redemption that we battle, and for Britain's resurrection that we strive. So, fight well for your God. Fight well for your country. And know that God will bless you all for your sacrifice.

'Please, sing with me, *Onward Christian soldiers*.'

***

Claypole and Stiles walked away from the hangar. Behind them, the priest re-packed his altar goods into their box.

'What are the orders of the day?' Stiles asked.

'They didn't send me any,' Claypole replied. 'Which means either there aren't any, or someone forgot to send them.' Claypole pursed his lips. 'I could chase them up' – he stopped and turned to gaze back at the men in the hangar – 'or I could leave it be. You know, give the riggers a chance to fix up the aircraft, give the pilots a chance to take a breather.'

Stiles smiled to himself.

'Well, knowing what a tight ship Lieutenant Colonel Beadle runs, I have absolute faith that the staff are operating at peak efficiency and all is as it should be,' Stiles said.

Claypole mirrored the other man's smile.

'Alright, Harry. Tell them they're on stand-by,' he said. 'But make it plain it's an early night for all. I need everyone at readiness by five o'clock tomorrow morning.'

Stiles diverted back to the hangar and Claypole strode on towards the farmhouse. As he reached the gate, the priest puttered past on his motorbike and accelerated away along the road. As Claypole reached the farmhouse door, a ragged cheer drifted across the airfield.

The Same Day – Beneath Arras

The sergeant trailed into the chamber and hunkered down in front of the platoon. He pulled off his helmet and scratched his scalp as card games stalled and faces turned towards him.

'Alright, lads?' he asked, and nodded briefly at the murmurs of affirmation that drifted from his soldiers. 'I've tried my level best to get us returned to our original assignment, but no-one seems to be able or willing to help.'

The soldiers met this news with resigned silence.

'So, we're in this one, whether we like it or not.' He pulled a thin smile. 'But if it wasn't this one, it would be the next one, so what's the difference in the end?' He looked around the pallid faces before him. 'Now, listen carefully.

'Jump-off is tomorrow at dawn, so we'll be moving out of this cave at 04:30. The Australians have been busy tunnelling out under our frontline; they'll blow exits and we'll be forming up in no man's land.'

One soldier released a low whistle of apprehension.

The sergeant pressed on: 'The barrage opens at 05:30 and the Aussies have set a couple of mines under the German lines that will go up at the same time. Stay exactly where you are' – he glanced around the faces once more to emphasise his point – 'because every single gun will be ranged on the German frontline, and that will feel pretty darn close to where you'll be lying.

'After three minutes the barrage will creep forward, one hundred yards every three minutes. You will get up and advance behind it. Keep your pace steady. Remember, the gunners can't see where you are, they are simply working to the clock.

'The barrage will take care of any Germans who are above ground. But watch out for dugouts and take care of them with grenades; you don't want Huns popping out of the earth behind you.

'The Canadians are assaulting the centre of the ridge; we're here to protect their right flank. So, be careful not to outrun them. Having said that, we're expected to make a major breakthrough on the ridge tomorrow. So, as long as you can see friendly troops on either side, it's probably wise to keep pushing forward.

'Right' – he stood up – 'four of you come with me to collect rations, bombs and ammunition. For the rest, there's a chaplain in one of the caves down yonder who is taking services for the rest of the day.' He smiled once more. 'Happy Easter.'

The sergeant left with his small party, and a few of the men pulled themselves to their feet to go in search of the sacrament.

'Are you going, Percy?' Charlie asked. 'To the service?'

Percy looked down at his boots.

'I don't think so,' he said. 'There's an awful lot of men that will be out there in the morning. God can't possibly save them all. Perhaps it's fairer if I just take the sporting chance.'

Charlie looked across to the chamber entrance and back to Percy's face.

'I think I'd like to go,' he said. 'Would you mind?'

Percy smiled: 'You go,' he said. 'You're too young to gamble.'

Chapter 15

04:45hrs – Easter Monday, 9 April 1917 – Beneath Arras

The lights flickered on, throwing a sickly sheen across the damp chamber walls. The dull electric buzz of the makeshift wiring was soon lost in the grunted complaints of rousing soldiers. Charlie stretched out his chilled and aching legs and hauled against his protesting backbone to sit upright on his sacking bed. He looked around at his waking companions. Their physical presence touched him with reassurance in the face of the gathering tug of events.

An officer stood at the entrance to the chamber, casting an appraising eye over the awakening men, and an orderly moved amongst the figures on the floor, dispensing rum into proffered tin mugs.

Charlie watched Percy swig his ration and flush it like a mouthwash around his teeth. The orderly poured Charlie's shot and moved on. Charlie sniffed at the smoky, dark liquid and followed Percy's example. The rum burned his gums, penetrating between his teeth and drying the enamel with its crude, overpowering hotness. Charlie's eyes streamed tears and he clamped his hand over his mouth, fighting his convulsions to avoid the humiliation of a cough. Percy caught his eye and winked.

The muffled bark of an explosion silenced the low mutterings in the chamber and a pulse of air pressure bulged against the men's ear-drums.

'Right!' The officer's voice drew all eyes towards him. 'The sappers have blown the exits. Prepare to move out.'

Soldiers lurched to their feet, wrapping mufflers, fastening greatcoats, squirming into the shoulder-straps of backpacks and retrieving rifles from pyramid stacks. Last cigarettes were lit and deep draws of smoke were sucked hungrily down rum-warmed throats.

'Whatever else' – Trevor looked around his four companions – 'we try to stick together. Agreed?'

The band of companions clasped each other's shoulders then fell to silence and turned, with all the others, to face the chamber entrance.

The officer leaned into the tunnel for a moment, waiting for the crush of moving men from other chambers to ease, then he turned back to address the soldiers.

'Keep it as quiet as you can. No cigarettes. No talking. Remember: Three minutes for every hundred yards.' He flashed a smile. 'Good luck. Let's go.'

The officer ducked out of the chamber and the infantrymen shuffled through the bottle-necked exit to follow him. The narrow tunnel forced the heavily-laden soldiers into single-file, each man's rifle held against his chest, pushed against the pack of the man in front. The tunnel meandered in slow curves to the left and the right. On either side, every few yards, an arch opened into a now-empty chamber littered with discarded ration tins and cigarette packets. Abruptly, another officer appeared ahead, blocking the way and directing the column of men at right-angles into a newly cut passageway, this one straight and unlit.

The soldiers' progress slowed, partly because of the pitch darkness, partly because of a crush developing ahead. A tendril of fresh breeze tickled across the men's faces, a portent of the chill pre-dawn air above them.

Shuffling along behind the sergeant, Percy led the group of friends, with Charlie pressed tight on his back. He craned his neck and caught a glimpse of dark sky, suddenly blotted from view by the bulky passage of a body.

'Where nearly out, lad,' he hissed over his shoulder. 'Ten more yards.'

The sharp tang of recently discharged cordite stung deep into Percy's sinuses as the tunnel's roof opened to the sky and the sergeant's body in front of him moved upwards sharply. He squinted down to see the muddied rung of a ladder and hoisted himself up its short length. He emerged into a desultory squall of frigid rain backed with the dull, everlasting rumble of the barrage dropping its persistent niggle of flashing disruption across the enemy-held horizon.

The officer from the chamber squatted in front of him, his right arm pointing away along the dark, fetid mud of no man's land.

'Move along to the end the line and lay down,' he hissed. 'Go quietly.'

Percy ducked left and followed the dark mass of the man before him, padding in a crouching walk along the line of mud-caked boots and sodden puttees of the prone soldiers lying in silence, facing the dispassionate darkness that draped the German front line.

Hundreds of yards of hobnailed cobblery slid by and Percy's bent back panged with the urgent desire to stand straight. At last, the sergeant dropped to the ground and Percy thankfully settled into the mud close by the man's side. Moments later, Charlie dropped next to him, then one by one, the others joined the line.

Percy rocked his hips and carefully pulled his bayonet from its scabbard. He settled flat on the ground and clicked the oiled blade onto the mounting lugs on his rifle-barrel. Charlie turned his bloodless face towards the sound, anxiety dancing in his eyes. Percy treated him to another wink. There was nothing else left to do.

Behind them, the faint squelching of boots on the soft earth continued as the ribbon of infantry unrolled along no man's land in the dark.

05:20hrs – Vert Galant

A sudden flurry of sleet lashed against the mess windows. Benn looked up from his breakfast of scrambled egg and tinned meat. His eyes itched with tiredness. He allowed them to close, rubbing his fingertips across his greasy eyelids, seeking respite from the discomfort.

Something ceased. Abruptly, an element of his environment fell away like a landslide and a fresh absence tugged at his senses. He opened his eyes and tilted his head, searching for whatever was no longer there. A weaker spatter of icy rain rattled the window and the gusting wind dropped away to momentary stillness.

'*The barrage has stopped.*' Benn whispered the words to himself, incredulous. He tilted his head the other way. A vacuum of soft silence had replaced the ubiquitous constancy of the British artillery.

'The barrage has stopped.' He said it louder.

Standing, he pulled his greatcoat from the back of the chair and swung it onto his shoulders. He walked to the window, cupping his hands to the glass to better see into the encroaching dawn. Then he went to the door and stepped outside.

Minton watched him go. He lit his pipe, retrieved his own greatcoat and followed.

On the duckboards in front of the mess, Benn gazed at the sky as if this fundamental change in his world might somehow become visible. The door creaked and clicked shut behind him and he turned to confront Minton.

'The barrage has stopped,' Benn said.

Minton nodded, cupping his palm over his pipe-bowl and drawing a lungful of smoke.

'I'll wager it's a trap,' he answered.

'I don't understand,' Benn said, returning his gaze to the sky. 'What do you mean, a trap?'

'Well, any German soldier who has survived these last five days has done so by getting as deep underground as he can.' Minton's pipe glowed a vibrant orange and the tobacco smoke swirled around his face and tore away on the blustering breeze. 'They've been safe and snug down there, 'cos they know our lads won't attack while the shells are falling.

'So, now…' He took a step forward and laid a hand on Benn's shoulder. 'Right now, as we speak, the Germans are scurrying up the ladders and steps, climbing at-the-double out of their dugouts and shelters. They're locking machine guns onto tripods and checking fields of fire. They're lining the fire-step, man next to man, with ammunition boxes open at their feet. They'll be watching through what's left of their wire and waiting. Because they know that the barrage only stops to let Tommy get over the top and walk across no man's land towards them. Except, this time-'

The air around their heads split apart; ripped, torn and shattered by the concussive thunder-clap of thousands of gun barrels flinging thousands of shells at the same instant into the grey void. Benn ducked instinctively, hunching his shoulders as if dodging an expected blow.

'Fuck!' His involuntary cry was swept away in the clattering cacophony that pulsed in waves against his face. He turned wide-eyed as more pilots spilled through the mess door, their faces drawn with astonishment that matched his own. Seconds later, the percussive bark of the artillery was overlain with the ragged rumble of explosions as the first volley of shells found their target, swelling the guns' hard-edged noise with its distant rippling counterpoint.

The boards beneath the men's feet jolted in sympathy to a shockwave that surged through the ground. A second convulsion followed, then the overwhelming roar of two unfathomably huge explosions caught up with the blasts that had birthed it, expunging for a moment the impossible din of the redoubled barrage from the pilots' ears, before echoing away between the sky and the land.

The pilots of Jackdaw Squadron stood aghast in the milky dawn, feebly grateful that, on this morning, the Devil had visited Hell upon the heads of others.

05:20hrs – No Man's Land

A solitary shell landed a few hundred yards to the soldiers' front. Its detonation flashed the cloud base into garish relief and the blast boomed its way past their ears. Behind it, a heavy silence slumped across the land. Beneath the silence, the cold grey dawn bled into the sky's outer edge.

'What's happening?' Charlie hissed.

'Shhh.' Percy held a finger to his lips, then touched his ear and pointed ahead. '*Listen*,' he mouthed.

Charlie strained his ears into the empty stillness. A faint bustle of movement resonated in the distance; the jangle of a chain against a tripod, the scuff of a leather sole on wooden duckboards, the chink of a breech closing over an ammunition belt: the tiny sounds of men who had no choice making ready to face what they could not predict.

Charlie's gaze remained fixed on Percy's face. Percy allowed a hint of a grin to creep into his features as he rolled his eyes to their rear in exaggerated anticipation.

Somewhere in the middle distance a lonely signal gun boomed. In the next instant the world was drowned in a deluge of clamouring noise that beat down on their heads and tore at their senses.

Percy shouted something into Charlie's face. Charlie could smell the other's fetid, rum-laced breath but his words were lost in the bedlam. Percy shifted his eyes to the front and Charlie followed his gaze in time to witness the arrival of the first shells.

Staggeringly close, in a line that stretched along the whole grey horizon, light and violence erupted like a continuous flash of sheet lightning constantly fed from above by salvo after salvo of shells.

The ground lurched under Charlie's stomach once, then again, the dread pulsing of massive destruction resonating through the earth, then the rumbling roar of two monstrous explosions rolled together across the battlefield like a solid ceiling of sound. Charlie pressed his cheek against the soil. Beyond Percy's hunched figure, the sergeant lay with his eyes fixed on his wristwatch with the calm concentration of an umpire. Charlie nailed his gaze to the other man's serenely concentrated face as the wild horses of Armageddon stamped and galloped across the sky above him.

Minutes that spanned eternities crawled past. Finally, the sergeant pulled himself up onto one knee, beckoning down the line for his soldiers to do likewise. Charlie hauled himself up, feeling for the first time the rain-soaked coarseness of his trousers chafe against his frigid legs.

The sergeant stared ahead, resolute amongst the pandemonium, waiting. Distress rockets fired from behind the German lines, desperate demands for artillery intervention that scratched glittering curves of gold and amber against the flashing backdrop of annihilation that stitched through the German trenches.

The barrage moved; its nearest detonations receded as its arching, probing fingers groped eastwards. The sergeant stood upright and began walking steadily towards the enemy. The soldiers to his right and left followed his lead.

Charlie stumbled upright onto legs numbed by cold and fear. He glanced to his left. Jack was next to him, then Trevor and Geordie, flanked by a long ribbon of men stretching into the distance. He looked right at Percy's wiry form bent to action, and the sergeant's wide frame, upright and solid. A wash of commonality pushed a heady warmth into his blood and he fixed his eyes on the tangled wire and smoking trenches ahead.

The sergeant strode towards a ragged gap in the wire. Men bunched behind and followed him, snaking through the breech. Bullets ripped the air and sparked like anger from the tangled metal coils. Charlie heard sharp cries behind him cutting through the din, but he swivelled his hips through the gap and fixed his eyes onto Percy's back.

The soldiers moved quicker now, spurred by the proximity of hostile opposition. Around him, men dropped to their knee, firing at shapes that bobbed above the German parapet. Charlie scampered on, fixed in his intent to stick with his pal.

Percy dropped into the trench and Charlie tumbled after him. Crumpled bodies lay on the wrecked parapet and the trench floor, crushed and contorted by explosive force. Away to his left, two British soldiers were bent over, thrusting bayonets into a writhing German. Their victim flapped in self-defence with bare, bloodied hands, his mouth stretched with his desperate cries for mercy. To Charlie's right, Percy darted away towards an entranceway hung with old potato sacks, Charlie dashed after him. Percy leaned against the trench wall next to the entrance and pulled a grenade from his greatcoat pocket. Charlie braced his legs and raised his rifle to his shoulder. Percy tossed the bomb down the dugout. A few moments later a hand grasped the edge of the sacking from the inside. Charlie fired three shots through the sack and the hand jerked back. The grenade exploded in the dugout, billowing the sack outwards in a bulge of smoke and dust. Percy shoved his rifle into the opening and loosed off a few rounds into the choking haze.

Wide eyed, Charlie stared at the bullet holes in the sack. The edge of his vision darkened and his stomach churned with a sickly dismay.

Abruptly, the sergeant loomed in front of Charlie and grabbed his shoulder. Leaning close to Charlie's face, the big man bellowed something inaudible and gesticulated over the trench wall, to the east, before lumbering off along the splintered duckboards. Charlie caught Percy's eye and saw a savage glee glinting there. He found himself grinning back and together they clambered up the earthen wall onto the slimy mud beyond.

06:00hrs – Vert Galant

Claypole pulled the orders out of the mud-stained message tube. He leafed through the cream-coloured papers, scanning the terse directives they conveyed.

'Right, gentlemen.' He raised his voice against the swelling din of artillery fire that rattled the farmhouse windows. 'It has begun, as I'm sure you've noticed. Our soldiers are now on the offensive. They will be advancing behind a very substantial creeping barrage. The British 3rd Army will be attacking out of Arras while the Canadian Corps secure the British left flank by capturing Vimy Ridge.'

'Good Lord,' Stiles breathed. 'Capture the ridge? That's a stretch.'

'Of course,' – Claypole ignored the intervention – 'the only way to manage such a fluid artillery plan is by aerial observation. The spotters will be out in force and we're tasked with protecting them. So, it will be a day of patrols in the general area from Arras to the town of Vimy. That patrol line straddles the expected advance of both armies.'

'But, sir' – Davenport glanced at the slush bedecked window – 'this weather is practically unflyable.'

'Yes, it is,' Claypole answered. 'But we'll get on better if you confine your observations to things that I can do something about. Now, what strength do you have left on your flights?'

'I have three,' Mumford said. 'Including me.'

'Also three,' Davenport answered quietly.

'Good,' Claypole said. 'How about you, Harry?'

'I can put up four,' Stiles replied.

'Then you go first,' Claypole said. 'As soon as you can.'

Stiles moved away to don his flying gear and Claypole turned to Hartley.

'What do you have?' he asked.

'No-one' – Hartley grimaced – 'except me.'

'Right. Then you'll fly with me,' Claypole said. He dropped the sheaf of orders onto the table. 'Let's get to it.'

06:10hrs – Approaching the German Second Line

The rain strengthened to sweeping belts of sleet as Percy and Charlie rolled over the back wall of the German trench and lay prone under the stinging jabs of icy rain. They looked across a landscape of overlapping shell-holes, a filthy honeycomb of steaming dank pits. The barrage marched on, whipping distant banks of wire into undulating convulsions, then dropping them and rampaging onwards.

Percy glanced left and right. On both sides, soldiers rolled and tumbled out of the enemy trench, clambered to their feet and pushed on. He nudged Charlie into motion. Slipping on the wet earth, they rose and stumbled forward, keeping to the thin tracery of ridges that formed a broken network of boundaries between the gaping shell-holes.

Men mingled around them, crossing and re-crossing their front as the crowd picked their way across the broken earth. Charlie gasped with sudden recognition as Trevor and Geordie melded into their path. Charlie looked beyond them, searching for Jack. Trevor clapped him on the shoulder in greeting and shook his head.

'Jack's gone,' he shouted, his words whipped away by the raging barrage as it pounded its colossal path away from them. 'Move! Move!'.

They skittered on along the slick, curving rims of earth, their breath rasping against the corrosive catch of cordite in the air. The sky lightened further as broad fingers of dawn squeezed in between the desolate overcast.

The long ribbon of advancing soldiers lapped into the rolls of barbed wire like a wave against a breakwater; stalled against the unbroken obstacle. Charlie dropped to his knee with the others, searching for a gap, a weakness that could be forced. Charlie looked down the line of men to his left. They were slumping to the ground, folding in on themselves. Sparks danced along the wire, dashing along its length towards him. He opened his mouth to shout.

Trevor's helmet spun away from his head. The force of the machine gun bullets dragged him to his feet and arched his body backwards in a stiff curve to drop like a log into the mud.

Charlie recoiled, lost his footing and slid backwards amidst the whipping buzz of malice scorching through the air around him. He landed heavily, upside down, in the shell-hole. Percy's face appeared briefly in front of his, then strong hands pulled him further into cover and helped him right himself.

Finding himself wedged between Percy and Geordie, Charlie gasped with shock. Blood hammered through his temples and he squeezed his eyes shut against the vision of Trevor's hollowed face and dangling jaw. He clenched his teeth and choked down a surge of revulsion that bulged in his throat. He slowed his breathing and forced himself to check his rifle barrel and breech for fouling.

Charlie felt his two companions ease their way up the shell-hole and he squirmed with them to peek over its ragged edge. Fifty yards behind the wire, close to the ground, the rectangular firing slit of a small concrete bunker sparkled with phrenetic muzzle-flash, traversing slowly from left to right, begetting metallic twinkles as its fire swept through the wire and over the bodies of the prone soldiers beyond

The three men ducked down as the hailstorm of bullets thrashed over them on its way down the line.

'I'll try to bomb them out!' Geordie was shouting hard, but his words were distant in the cacophony. 'Cover me!'

They waited for the gun to sweep back the other way, then Geordie slipped off his pack and slithered over the edge of the shell-hole towards the wire.

The passing barrage had lifted the coils and dumped them back onto themselves. A section was rucked up on itself, creating a small gap against the ground where it was creased. Squirming onto his back, Geordie began wriggling his way under this gap. Percy and Charlie aimed their rifles at the dancing light of the German muzzle, firing and reloading, firing and reloading.

They ducked again as the German bullets swept back and lashed over their heads. When they resumed firing, Geordie had vanished beyond the wire. Percy squeezed off a few more rounds before a movement to the right of the bunker caught his eye. He nudged Charlie to stop firing.

The movement resolved into a figure, flat against the ground, edging forward on the bunker's flank. Percy looked down the line to see riflemen firing from shell-holes and folds in the ground.

'They don't know Geordie's out there,' he shouted at Charlie. Then: 'Stop firing!'

His cries floundered in the chatter of the German gun and the rumble of the unending artillery. The pair ducked again as the stream of bullets scythed once more past their hiding place. Pulling themselves back up to the edge they saw Geordie haul himself onto the bunker roof, lean over its front face and deposit two Mills bombs through the slit.

Two detonations belched smoke and dust from the aperture and the gun fell silent, its barrel swinging upwards to rest against the blackened concrete.

Soldiers scrambled from shell-holes on the left and right, some wielding wire-cutters. Gaps were cut and men squirmed through towards the enemy trenches beyond. Percy and Charlie pulled themselves upright, their gaze locked on the unmoving figure sprawled on the hard concrete pad.

'Come on, lad.' Percy shouted directly into Charlie's face. 'Let's not waste it.'

They joined with the last of the soldiers squeezing through a gap in the wire. Ahead of them, the stifled explosions of grenades in dugouts and the occasional crack of a rifle marked the neutralising of the remaining defenders.

Percy and Charlie walked the last few dozen yards to the German second line slowly, shoulder to shoulder through the tumbling rain. They dropped over the parapet into the wide-cut trench. Stepping over grey-clad bodies, they made their way in the direction of the machine gun nest. As they drew near, two soldiers passed Geordie's limp body down into the trench. The men that received the body laid it gently along the trench wall and spread a groundsheet over it. To the east, the barrage marched on and its noise dropped away.

'Thirty minutes rest here while the Canadians cross our front,' a disembodied voice echoed through the new quietness. 'Then we press on to the ridge.'

07:30hrs – Vert Galant

Sleet squalls lashed across the airfield as the late, weather-darkened dawn crawled towards mid-morning. Returning Pups wobbled their way back to land, buffeted by the savage cross-wind, while others hauled themselves into the ragged air and banked east to take their places. Men on the ground moved around the stationary aircraft in the stiff-limbed fashion imposed by heavy, rain-sodden clothing, passing petrol cans and ammunition belts between chilled-blue hands with red-raw knuckles. Pilots stood in pairs or alone, waiting in desultory silence for their turn to fly, numbed by both the cold and the preponderous weight of the moment.

Claypole and Hartley emerged from the farmhouse and started across the field. Claypole spied Stiles standing on his Pup's wing-root, leaning forward and wiping the moisture from his gun with an oily rag.

'Harry!' he called, beckoning the man over.

Stiles jumped to the ground and loped across to meet his commander.

'What does it look like out there?' Claypole asked.

Stiles had kept his googles on to cheat the gusting sleet and, together with his greasy, stocking-covered face, they created a deeply alien countenance from which his familiar voice chirped with unexpected optimism.

'It's going bloody well, as far as I could tell.' He raised his voice against the twin impediments of engine noise from taxiing biplanes and the Vaseline slicked silk stretched over his mouth. 'There are men on the move along the entire line. They're close-up behind the barrage, mopping up as they go. The German artillery are shelling our empty trenches, so they obviously have no idea what's coming their way.'

'In the air, Harry? What's going on in the air?' Claypole said.

'Ah, yes. Our spotter chaps are scuttling about quite nicely,' Stiles said. 'I've seen one or two go down to ground fire. But they're having to fly low; you can't see the ground at all if you're much above three-hundred.'

'And the Germans?' Claypole asked.

'Saw a few, but they were playing it cagey and didn't bother us at all. It might be different if you were flying alone.'

'Thanks, Harry. Carry on.'

Claypole strode off with renewed vigour towards the hangar and Hartley scrambled to catch up.

'We'll take a look behind the German lines,' Claypole announced, half over his shoulder. 'There might be some trouble we can stir up there.'

07:45hrs – Approaching Vimy Ridge

Charlie and Percy dropped to a crouch as machine gun fire flared up ahead, close enough to make them cautious, too distant to invoke concern. They took the moment to rest and look around.

The ground sloped gently upwards and quickly crested to form the southern end of Vimy Ridge. The platoon had leeched into the Canadian Division on their left and were straggling behind their advance. The dead and wounded they passed bore Canadian patches, and Canadian stretcher-bearers moved among them.

The machine gun chops echoed across the hillside for another minute before ending in the sharp detonations of several grenades. A salvo of shells creased the air above and stitched a ragged line of explosions across the enemy positions on the crest.

'Come on, Charlie,' Percy said. 'Let's get on, but let's go careful.'

08:00hrs – Over Arras

Claypole's Nieuport ploughed through the swirling sleet, staying low to keep sight of the landmarks he needed to find his way forward. Eventually a thick ribbon of undulating flashes sketched itself across the landscape – the muzzle-flashes of the massed British artillery – and beyond that, the ragged skyline of Arras, its buildings pitted and holed by the violence that had raged around them for year after weary year.

Claypole zig-zagged a path between gun emplacements, set a course to cross the south-eastern part of the city, and pulled into a shallow climb.

Once past Arras, he modulated his altitude to maintain sight of the ground whilst retaining the protective cloak of the murk, abandoning any precision in navigation to the quivering pointer on his compass. He glanced back over his right shoulder to see the snow-blurred outline of Hartley's Pup sitting wide off his starboard side as they crossed what had been, until that morning, the frontline.

Smoke and vapour rolled with the wind across the battleground below, a storm that mirrored the weather that roiled above it. Flares arced from one domain into the other, their brightness sucked away by the wet air, the frantic urgency of their unknown entreaties muffled and lost in the low-hanging snow-laden clouds.

Through the gaps in this misty obfuscation, Claypole glimpsed the movements of men: second or third waves of fighting infantry toiling forward, groups of prisoners trailing back and stretcher parties moving through the inert bodies that lay in lines afront the enemy trenches and the machine gun nests.

As they slogged north-east, the ground ahead glittered with a wavering phosphorescence that grew brighter as they approached. The ragged explosions of the barrage, their blast muted by his engine's roar, their flashing violence diffused by the misty air, looked no more dangerous than fireworks in a November sky. They flew on, protected from aerial ambush by a blanketing layer of cloud.

Assuming they had entered enemy territory, Claypole scanned the ground for something to attack. Nothing moved and no feature attracted attention on the barren, suppurating soil that had been heaved and re-heaved by many days of artillery bombardment.

Flares curved into the sky over to Claypole's left where Vimy Ridge tumesced from the flat plain. The Canadians were well forward; the realisation stabbed a jolt of excitement through his loins. The southern end of the ridge pulled the land upwards beneath his wheels, stealing his altitude even while he flew level. Sudden movement dotted the ground below him. Khaki shapes loped up the slope, paused to fire and pushed ahead. Mills bombs popped in short flashing bursts and fixed bayonets gleamed in the sullen daylight.

Claypole topped the ridge at 100ft and found the shattered remains of a wood blanketing the back slope, the rushing blur of splintered branches hiding whatever might be concealed amongst them. Claypole peered ahead through the shimmering disc of his propeller, beyond the woodland's edge to the clear slope behind, and his heart leapt.

Grey-clad figures led several teams of six horses up the gentle slope towards a crescent of artillery pieces that other men were readying to withdraw. Claypole dropped his wing as he overflew the emplacement and saw that one gun had already been hitched to its horse-team. Gritting his teeth, he hauled back on the stick sending his aircraft up into a loop, climbing into the murk. At the loop's apex, he half-rolled the right way up and dove back towards the German position, lining up on the cannon that was being hauled into motion.

Claypole squeezed the trigger and his machine gun juddered into action. Bullets flailed through the air, chopped into the backs of the last pair of horses and lashed across the gun's breech and barrel. Claypole flashed overhead, banking to assess his attack.

The other teams of horses on the hillside broke and bolted down the slope. Their handlers sprinted and dived for the cover of the woods. The four still-living beasts on the hitched team lurched and reared in panic against the dead weight of the shot pair, kicking and biting each other to get free.

Muzzle flashes peppered the wood's dark edge as the artillery crews rallied what small defence they could. Claypole banked over the woods to avoid their attention and looked around for his wingman. Hartley flew alongside him, pointing with an exaggerated motion at his machine gun and shaking his head. Claypole nodded his understanding and pointed west before climbing to find the cover of cloud base for the journey home.

08:20hrs – Approaching the Third Line

Bullets hissed through the damp air, forcing the soldiers onto their bellies and compressing their progress against the bulwark of the final German line. Enemy machine gunners commanded the slope and lashed any movement with fire.

Percy and Charlie lay stretched out on their backs against the forward slope of a shallow shell-hole. The body of a previous occupant slumped over its lip and the flat thwack of bullets into flesh showed his corpse was still attracting attention from the trench-line ahead.

Two British biplanes roared overhead, flying east. Charlie bent his neck backwards to watch them pass.

'I told you to volunteer as a pilot,' Percy said. 'Better to be zooming about up there than wallowing in this shit pit.'

A salvo of shells crashed onto the ridge, dropping their sudden violence appallingly close. The explosions echoed away to be replaced with an upswell of shouts and the brittle crackling of rifle fire.

'Crickey,' Percy said. 'They're storming it. The bloody Canadians are storming it.'

The two men scrabbled up on either side of the dead body and peered over the edge. The slope was alive with soldiers loping the last few yards and dropping over the enemy parapet. Charlie looked at Percy over the soldier's torso. Percy nodded and they scrambled onto their feet and trotted forward.

Men dotted the hillside and calls for stretcher-bearers rang through the air. The rattle of rifle shots along the trench-line diminished and fell silent. Percy and Charlie jogged the last few yards through the sharp haze of fresh cordite and dropped over the shell-shattered parapet.

'We've done it, Percy,' Charlie gasped. 'We got right through to the end.'

Percy glanced up and down the trench at the milling Canadians clasping hands and slapping backs.

'I'm not sure it's safe just yet,' Percy said. 'What if the artillery doesn't receive word and has another pop at the trench-line?'

A long burst of machine gun fire in the distance followed by a smattering of rifle shots quelled the celebrations in the trench and soldiers began to climb out by the back wall.

'Come on, Charlie,' Percy said. 'Best we stick with the crowd.'

They clambered out of the trench and walked eastwards, ducking briefly in alarm as the two biplanes barrelled overhead in the opposite direction.

For one hundred yards or more the ground behind the trench was as shell-churned as the land to its front. Then splintered clumps of tree-stumps gave way to chewed-up trunks that leaned at varying angles away from the trench. Further on, the trunks stood taller with splinter-lopped branches, their wounds bleeding the amber scent of sap into the still air to compete with the damp fug of rotting pine needles.

The line of soldiers, with rifles poised, moved deeper into the damaged wood, cracking twigs under their boots as they advanced. Charlie glanced left and right cautious of outpacing the advance. Reassured, he looked ahead into the gloom between the trees.

The forest floor glittered with pin-pricks of light and something buzzed through the air, knocking his right leg away from under him. Halfway through his pirouette to the ground, the harsh bark of rifles reached his ears. He hit the ground hard and three more bullets slashed through the air over his body. He gasped against empty lungs, struggling to drag oxygen back into his chest, wincing against the bolts of pain that lanced up his leg.

Shouts filled the air as soldiers crashed forward and volleys of rifle-fire rippled through the woods. Charlie lifted his head cautiously; he was alone, and the shouts and gunfire grew more distant. Emboldened, he sat up to check his wound. Immediately a wave of woozy nausea granulated his vision; the lower half of his shin sat at right-angles to his leg and the toe of his boot was pointing at his face.

Charlie slumped backwards onto the damp carpet of pine needles as waves of amplifying pain pulsed up through his groin. He clenched his teeth and stared into the flat grey sky through the canopy of wounded, broken branches.

08:45hrs – Vert Galant

Claypole slid his biplane down through the cape of drizzle that hung over the airfield. He curved into the buffeting breeze and dropped the aircraft onto the grass for a perfect landing. Zig-zagging across the turf, he taxied to the hangar doors and switched off the engine. Riggers pulled on their greatcoats and came out to take charge of the fighter.

'Take her inside,' Claypole said to the nearest of the groundcrew. 'I've finished for the day.'

He stood and watched the men haul the Nieuport away, admiring the sparkle that the raindrops coaxed from its silvered fuselage. He turned to see Hartley trudging back to the farmhouse and set off to converge with him.

Hartley glanced up as the other man drew alongside, then his eyes dropped again to the slush-riven turf.

'What happened?' Claypole asked.

'My bloody gun jammed,' Hartley replied. 'No more than half-a-dozen bullets down the belt and the bloody thing locked solid. I gave it a good thumping but there was no joy to be had. We had those gun teams cold. I could've done some real damage there.'

'Can't be helped,' Claypole said. 'In any event, it will take them hours to chase down those horses, and the Canadians were on the other side of the ridge, moving forward. I'll bet my eye-teeth it didn't end well for the gun crews.'

'That's as may be,' Hartley sighed. 'But it's a long way to go and not get any real sport out of it.'

09:00hrs – Farbus Wood

Charlie's muscles quaked and shivered beyond his ability to control them. His sodden clothes lay heavy on his body, relentlessly leeching the warmth from his numbed flesh. Each involuntary shudder sparked jolts of electric pain from his broken leg and squeezed tears of impotent frustration from his eyes.

The rifle-shots had ceased several minutes ago and now the damp silence weighed on his mind as heavily as his wet greatcoat pressed on his chest. He considered shouting for help, but who would hear him? Who had won the skirmish in the wood? Who would get to him first?

Charlie closed his eyes, steadied his breathing and stayed quiet.

The soft crunch of boots on pine-needles floated through the tree-stilled air. The purposeful tread grew nearer, quickening as it came.

'Charlie?' Percy's voice was taught with concern.

Charlie exhaled a burst of relief: 'For Christ's sake, Percy. You put the bloody wind up me!'

Percy knelt down and looked at the other's disfigured leg.

'Are you hit anywhere else?' he asked.

'Not that I can feel,' Charlie answered.

'Right.' Percy leaned forward. 'This'll hurt.'

Percy pulled and straightened the broken leg; Charlie's howl of pain echoed through the pine trunks.

'Shush now,' Percy said. 'All done.'

He unhooked the shoulder-strap from Charlie's rifle and wrapped it around Charlie's thigh as a tourniquet.

'You should've been there, Charlie,' Percy enthused as he worked. 'There's half-a-dozen artillery pieces just beyond the edge of the wood. Big howitzers, dug into proper emplacements. Their crews put up a bit of a fight, but there were too many of us.' Percy's eyes glittered with pride. 'We've captured their guns, Charlie. You, me and the Canadians. We've captured their fucking guns!'

PART 3

SPIRAL

Chapter 16

Tuesday, 10 April 1917 – Vert Galant

As dawn broke, the air danced with the heavy softness of cascading snow. It muffled the metallic clank of spanners on engines and it subdued the shouts and calls of the mechanics. It smoothed out the bark of ignition as an engine was run up, and it dampened the rumble of the artillery fire that still rolled in from the east. It settled in the ruts and footprints on the field and it filled the sky with swirling curtains that spiralled down from the blue-black clouds.

Claypole and Stiles stood by the window of the farmhouse gazing at the snowfall.

'It's April' – Stiles shook his head slowly – 'and along comes the worst snow of the year.'

'Does it look flyable, Harry?' Claypole asked. 'I think it might *just* be flyable. What do you think?'

Both men turned at the clumping of boots on the wooden floor. Davenport, clad in full flying gear walked to the door and grasped the handle. He paused and met the gaze of the other two.

'Engine test,' he said through the layered wrap of his wool muffler. 'A couple of circuits and back down.'

He opened the door and exited amid a flurry of fat snowflakes. Claypole and Stiles looked at each other and moved to retrieve their own greatcoats.

'Davenport's a solid enough pilot,' Claypole said as he wound his scarf around his neck and pulled on his gloves. 'He'll tell us the score.'

The two men left the farmhouse, treading carefully on the slippery steps. The road had borne enough overnight traffic to pummel the snow to slush and melt the slush to mud. They stepped over the water-filled wheel ruts and followed Davenport's footprints onto the field. They stopped and waited as Davenport climbed into a distant Pup and the groundcrew hauled it around to face into the wind. Claypole's gaze drifted away from the lone scout on the field and he surveyed the sky, sucking in his cheeks like a mariner judging an undertow.

Stiles cleared his throat: 'I think it might not be,' he said quietly.

Claypole looked at him from beneath a frown: 'Might not be what?'

'Flyable,' Stiles said.

Claypole turned his head to watch the Pup accelerate across the field and lift gently into the air. Immediately its outline softened, then its dun green fuselage leeched to white, and at 100ft it vanished from view leaving only the cackling echo of its engine reaching back through the cocooning snow. Claypole stared at the point in the sky that had last held Captain Davenport and his biplane, listening as the engine noise receded to a muffled buzz that melted slowly into a chill silence.

Claypole's features darkened and his jaw tensed. Like a schoolmaster daring his pupils to defy him, his eyes bored into the snowstorm. Then his shoulders sagged and his chin fell to his chest.

'Fucking weather,' he muttered. 'Bloody, fucking weather.'

Wednesday, 11 April 1917

The rattle of the despatch rider's motorbike drew Stiles from his breakfast. He reached the door before the young soldier had a chance to knock, and took the message tube from him. Stiles watched the man ride away, the rear wheel of the begrimed cycle slewing through the muddy slush as it accelerated down the road. His gaze switched to the morning sky. The clouds still hung heavy and grey but without the gravid darkness of yesterday. He closed the door and went back to his meal, laying the despatches on the table by Claypole's elbow.

'The weather's better,' Stiles said. 'Not ideal, but definitely better.'

Claypole grunted his acknowledgement as he opened the message tube. He read through the scraps of paper, dropping each on the table as he finished it.

As he continued with his breakfast, Stiles noticed that his commander had stilled his movements and was holding one of the papers in front of his unfocussed eyes.

'What's up?' he asked.

'They've found Davenport,' Claypole replied. 'It seems he tried to set his plane down. I assume he believed he was landing on a road. Turns out it was a river.'

'Good Lord,' Stiles breathed. 'Is he badly hurt?'

'Broken nose and broken back.' Claypole dropped the slip of typed paper onto the pile.

Hartley and Mumford drifted across and sat at the table.

'They've shipped him back to a dressing station,' Claypole continued. 'From there he'll be on the next available boat to England.'

A silence pressed on the group, heavy and uncomfortable.

'I'm glad he's alive,' Claypole ventured into the hush. 'He's a good man, a decent pilot. Is he married?'

'No, sir,' Stiles said. 'I don't think he was the marrying kind.'

The silence slumped back. Claypole looked down and shuffled through the papers, pulling one from the small pile and holding it up.

'In any event, our work goes on.' He looked around the three drawn faces, waiting for eye contact from each before moving to the next, methodically reasserting control. 'This morning, the offensive has been renewed. Monday's gains pushed the enemy off the high ground, so they've lost the commanding view that they've enjoyed for so long. Because of that, I suspect they'll have plenty of spotters in the air.

'I'm told' – he waved the paper in emphasis – 'that we cannot expect replacement pilots until early next week. So, we need to make do with what we have. You' – he pointed at Hartley – will take over Davenport's pilots. That gives us three flights to rotate on patrol. Harry, you take the first one up. Any questions?'

Stiles stood up to prepare for his patrol, the scrape of his chair was the only sound in the room.

***

Stiles strode across the field towards the pilots' mess. Even in full flying kit, the atmosphere's damp cold crept into his bones. He kicked at the hardy meadow grass that tufted through the vestigial ribbons of crystallising snow. It was more grey than green; stuck in its enforced dormancy, waiting with insentient patience for spring to arrive.

Stiles opened the door to the mess.

'Platt, Potter, Morris,' he called into the room. 'We take off on patrol in ten minutes.' He made to leave.

'Sir? If I may? What news of Captain Davenport?'

Stiles turned back to confront Minton's face, lined with concern.

'Yes, of course.' Harry's cheeks reddened at his omission, unseen under his silk mask. 'We only just received the despatches. He tried to land, er, away from the airfield, and things didn't turn out too well.'

'Was he badly hurt?' Minton asked.

'Enough to get his ticket home,' Stiles said. 'So, you and Lieutenant Clamp will fly with Captain Hartley for the moment.'

Stiles waited for a reply, but Minton just nodded sadly and turned away. Stiles glanced around the other faces that watched him, round and pale, like owls in a loft. He retreated, closed the door and walked to the hangar.

As he entered the hangar, he held up four fingers to the groundcrew. Men started into motion, manhandling and manoeuvring biplanes towards the field. Stiles wandered over to a glowing brazier and stretched his un-gloved fingers over its rippling warmth. He studied his hands, bleached white by the cold, with dark blue veins straddling their backs. He flexed his fingers, inciting a rush of pins-and-needles that made the freezing digits feel like sausages stuffed with sand. He rubbed his hands together to banish the sensation. Davenport intruded unbidden into his mind; Davenport in a bath-chair, Davenport with unfeeling, unmoving legs.

Stiles turned abruptly from the brazier. The crew were hauling the last of the four Pups through the hangar door, so he walked back to the pilots' mess and stood outside to await his pilots.

A few minutes later the door opened and Platt emerged with Potter close behind him. Both men nodded to their flight leader in passing. The gesture belied their usual cheerful demeanour. Stiles sighed and waited. Moments later, Morris emerged.

'Morning, sir,' Morris mumbled.

'Have you thought about what I said the other day?' Stiles asked. 'We can't carry on this way, less so now we're understrength. Jackdaw is a fighting squadron, so you have to fight.'

Morris remained silent.

'If things don't change' – Stiles placed a hand on the other's shoulder – 'I'm not sure what Major Claypole might do.'

'Well, that's the point, sir,' Morris said. 'I will have to answer to a higher authority than the major.'

'Listen to me. I'm a good Christian man' – Stiles reached inside his sheepskin and pulled out a black leather book – 'and this book of psalms was given to me by my good Christian wife. Reading this book has helped me reconcile the things I've had to do in this war with the life I lived before it and, God willing, I will one day go back to.' He pressed the book against the other man's chest. 'I want you to have it, so that it might help you in the same way.'

Morris took the book and pushed it into his pocket.

'You're a Christian soldier,' Stiles squeezed the other's shoulder. 'You *will* be forgiven.'

Engines coughed into life on the field behind them.

'Thank you for the book, Captain Stiles,' Morris said and walked away towards his aircraft.

Thursday, 12 April 1917

The dawn broke behind an obfuscating shroud of snowflakes pirouetting down in blue-white spirals to blanket the airfield in enforced idleness.

'What's that you're reading?'

Morris looked up into Potter's face. Potter stood unnaturally close beside the armchair, looming over him.

'It's a book of psalms,' Morris said. 'Captain Stiles gave it to me.'

Platt appeared, leaning on the back of the chair.

'Captain Stiles is a kind man,' he said, leering over Morris' shoulder. 'Some might say a bit too kind.'

Morris closed the book and laid it in his lap.

'What do you want with me?' he asked.

Potter crouched down in one swift movement, thrusting his face close.

'We want from you, only what we ourselves are giving.' Potter kept his voice low but it held an edge of menace. 'We are fighting for our God and country. That's the very same God that terrifies you with the prospect of His judgement' – Potter's eyes narrowed and his voice dropped to a hiss – 'and He will visit that very same judgement upon us.'

Platt slid down to crouch on the other side of the armchair, leaning in close on the other cheek.

'Here's the thing,' Platt said. 'We don't see any reason why we should carry you, God willing, to victory, when you're just play-acting to get by.'

'I thought I'd be able to do it,' Morris said. 'Believe me, I have tried.'

'Well,' – Potter jabbed a finger into Morris' chest to emphasise each word – 'try a bit fucking harder.'

Platt and Potter melted away and Morris squeezed the book in his lap like a sailor grips a lifeline.

***

Stiles stood by the window, watching the snow tumbling down with vacant detachment.

'How's your priest-boy progressing?' Claypole's voice cut into his reverie.

'I'm working on him.' Stiles didn't turn to give his answer. 'It's a sensitive process. He's a decent pilot and a good man at his core. I think it will work out.'

'It had better, Harry,' Claypole said. 'I can't, and won't, tolerate passengers. Especially now we're undermanned.'

A dark shape nosed through the settling snow on the road and drew to a halt outside the farmhouse.

'Are we expecting visitors?' Stiles asked.

'Not that I'm aware,' Claypole said.

'Well, a socking great staff car has just pulled up outside.'

'Shit!' Claypole cursed under his breath, scrabbling to fasten the buttons on his tunic.

Stiles moved away from the window, feigning interest in something on the stove-top. Hartley and Mumford stood up from their armchairs, as if sitting around was suddenly unpatriotic.

The door swung open and Lieutenant Colonel Tarquin Beadle strode in amongst a flurry of instantly melting snowflakes. His orderly followed close behind and shut the door.

'At ease, gentlemen.' Beadle grimaced his facsimile of a smile around the room. 'What a pleasure to see you all again. No operations today?'

'Er, no, sir,' Claypole answered. 'The weather is set against us, sir.'

'Ah.' Beadle nodded sagely. 'Perhaps tomorrow. Shall we sit?'

Beadle took the seat at the head of the table; the four other men took seats along the sides. Beadle's orderly stepped forward and handed him a slim sheaf of papers from a briefcase.

'First things first,' Beadle began. 'Monday was a jolly fine showing. Our friends, the Canadian Corps, captured Vimy Ridge in three hours. Can you believe that?' Beadle shook his head in affected bewilderment. 'Considering, two years ago, the French spent over three months running up and down that hill to no real benefit whatsoever. There are empires' – he shuffled through the papers as he muttered to himself – 'and there are *empires*.'

He found the document he sought.

'All objectives met on the day, ten thousand prisoners and fifty guns captured. A resounding success all round.' He pursed his lips. 'Sadly, on Tuesday, the weather, as you so neatly put it just now, was set against us. By the time we got back on the front foot, yesterday, the Germans had moved up sufficient reinforcements to hold us where we were, and that is currently still where we are.'

'What happens next, sir? Claypole asked.

'Well,' – Beadle leaned back in his chair – 'those better versed in military tactics tell me that advancing *down* a slope holds almost as many dangers and pit-falls as advancing *up* a slope. So, we intend to hold the line for a few days to keep the Germans occupied while we wait for the French to launch their offensive further south. General Nivelle is confident he has a plan that will drive the Germans out of France.'

The four other men stayed silent.

'In any event' – Beadle leaned forward again – 'I really came here on more important business. The French have asked the RFC to supply a small contingent of men to witness an execution. I've considered the matter carefully and decided I'd like Jackdaw Squadron to have the honour of providing four or five pilots for the purpose.'

'An execution?' Stiles couldn't hide his shock.

'Yes. Unpleasant business, I grant you, but there's been an element of dissent in the French lines recently,' Beadle said.

'Are you talking about mutiny, sir?' Claypole asked.

'Not really.' Beadle put his elbows on the table and interlaced his fingers. 'The French soldiers are apparently willing to defend their own trenches and repulse any German advance, but they have a growing reluctance to go over the top and participate in an assault. Which is obviously not very helpful in the week leading up to a major French offensive.'

Beadle retrieved another paper from his bundle and scanned it.

'It appears they've convicted two men. They're particularly keen to make the application of justice as visible as is seemly so that it may serve as a back-straightener for the whole French army in particular and for allied morale in general.'

'So, these men are not even deserters?' Stiles asked.

Beadle glanced at the paper again.

'Conspirators,' Beadle said. 'They have been convicted of *conspiring* to mutiny.' Beadle pursed his lips and looked directly at Stiles. 'What you must understand, Captain' – his voice hardened a degree – 'is that the enemy of victory is not one deserter here or two deserters there. No, the enemy of victory is the *infection* of men's minds with the *notion* that desertion is an option. There's only one way to crush that, and it has to be swift, decisive and final.'

'When is it to take place?' Claypole asked.

Beadle pushed the paper across the table to the other man.

'On Saturday, at first light.'

***

Stiles stood in the pilots' mess with Mumford slightly to one side and behind him. A hush hung over the assembled men, placed there by the news of the required witness party that Stiles had just delivered.

'Myself and Captain Mumford have volunteered to lead the party,' Stiles said. 'We need three more to make up the numbers.' He regarded the stony faces arrayed before him. 'Are there any volunteers?'

No-one moved a muscle. Stiles allowed the silence to extend for a few moments.

'I thought that might be the case' – Mumford stepped up next to him and held out an inverted sheepskin flying helmet – 'so I've prepared lots.'

Stiles reached into the helmet, pulled out a scrap of paper and unfolded it.

'Lieutenant Benn.'

Benn drew a sharp intake of breath, as if he'd been pinched, then hung his head to hide the twitching that invaded his cheek muscles.

Stiles dipped again into the helmet and retrieved a second name.

'Lieutenant Minton.'

Minton remained still, the unfocusing of his gaze his only reaction.

Stiles picked out the last witness.

'Second Lieutenant Morris.'

An exhalation of relief shuddered from the unpicked pilots. Morris raised his face to the rafters and closed his eyes.

Stiles scrunched the three papers together and dropped them back into the helmet.

'Those named will be excused duties tomorrow,' he announced. 'The party will muster in this mess at 04:00 hours on Saturday. That's all.'

Stiles and Mumford left the mess and trudged back towards the farmhouse. The snow churned around their heads with renewed vigour.

Chapter 17

Friday, 13 April 1917

Sometime overnight the snow had cooled to rain and the crystalline crust that overlaid the grass had retreated under the battering of raindrops. As dawn pushed towards mid-morning, the rain regressed to a misty drizzle that moved in broad swathes across the field.

Captain Hartley stood inside the doorway of the pilots' mess, venting his impatience via a slowly tapping foot, while Platt, Potter and Clamp finished pulling on their flying gear. When ready, they trooped past their flight leader into the damp air outside. Hartley swept a scornful glance across the three men remaining in the room, then swept out after his pilots, shutting the door with more force than was necessary.

Benn raised himself from his chair, drawn to the window by the simple, everlasting compulsion to watch aeroplanes taking off. The chug and cough of each starting engine joined together into a throaty chorus which transmuted to a roar as the flight of four Pups hauled away from the field and banked eastwards.

'That's it,' Benn said, craning his neck to stare after the receding formation. 'Half of what's left of Jackdaw Squadron is heading over the lines to risk their necks against the enemy while the other half sits in the warm with orders to have an early night so we're clear-eyed tomorrow morning to witness the French murdering their own soldiers.'

'It's not murder.' Minton's tobacco-frayed voice was quiet but firm. 'It's justice, handed down by a court-martial.'

Benn turned from the window and regarded the older man.

'No' – he shook his head slowly – 'once you're accused of mutiny, there's no officer on the whole western front who'll bother to look for reasons to say you're innocent. It's the kiss of death. The very accusation itself is the kiss of death.'

Minton scratched his chin for a moment, then reached into his pocket for his pipe.

'It's not a soldier's place to decide which orders to obey. It's not in a soldier's gift to argue the finer points of tactics with his superior officers,' Minton said. 'The moment he *does* stand up to question orders, it's all but certain that the question springs from a wish that he didn't have to carry them out. And that wish comes from a fear of what that order, that action, might mean for him personally. At that moment, in the eyes of the military, that soldier becomes a coward.'

'What about him?' Benn pointed at Morris on the other side of the room. 'Doesn't that make him a coward?'

Minton glanced across at Morris, his gaze lingering a moment as if in evaluation.

'No.' He turned back to face Benn. 'You and I both know what it takes to get into a plane and take it out on patrol. That young lad has never once baulked at an order to fly. He takes off, makes the same patrol as the rest of his flight, facing the same dangers. Up 'til now he's been lucky enough to come home when others haven't. Regardless, he's ready to do it the next day, and the next.'

'But he doesn't shoot at anything!' Frustration reddened Benn's cheeks.

'So' – Minton shrugged his shoulders – 'he's not a very useful soldier. That doesn't mean he's not a courageous soldier.'

Saturday, 14 April 1917

Stiles arranged a line of five tin mugs on a mess-room table and pulled the cork from an earthenware vessel. He poured a generous measure of dark liquid into each enamelled container. The pilots emerged from the dormitory, subdued by both the early hour and the prospect of the day's task.

'Rum,' Stiles announced by way of greeting. He and Mumford picked up their mugs. 'King George,' Stiles toasted and knocked back the spirit.

'The King,' Mumford seconded and follow suit.

The three pilots took up their mugs and mumbled acquiescence.

Mumford launched into a fit of choking coughs and Stiles turned to stare at him.

'I don't drink,' Mumford wheezed, wiping away the tears that tumbled down his cheeks.

Stiles watched the other man with bemusement until the convulsions quietened.

'Alright, lads,' – he turned back to the pilots – 'it's not a pleasant thing we have to do today, but it's also not a *difficult* thing. We just need to stand straight, look dead ahead and, when it's all done with, leave quietly, with respect.'

He turned and led them to the door. Outside a covered truck stood with its engine idling, wrapped in a thin mist of its own exhaust that condensed around its wheels in the cold pre-dawn air. Mumford swung into the driving seat and Stiles clambered in next to him. The others climbed into the back, pulled up the tailgate and secured it closed on its chains.

The three pilots sat on the fixed benches that ran down each side. Minton and Morris sat together on one side; Benn faced them on the other.

'I feel sick,' Benn said.

'That's rum on an empty stomach,' Minton said. 'You'll feel better when it's out of your guts and into your blood.'

'No' – Benn shook his head – 'it's a different sick; it's a hollow, empty sort of sick.' He looked into Minton's eyes. 'What's going to happen when we get there?'

'It's a firing squad, lad,' Minton said. 'It isn't complicated.'

Benn bowed his head and put a hand over his mouth, swallowing hard against the burning in his belly.

'Focus on a space slightly above everyone's head.' Minton pulled a thin smile of reassurance. 'That way you don't have to see anything.'

Benn retched once behind his hand, swallowing back the bile.

'I don't want to do this,' he said quietly. 'I really don't want to do this.'

Morris straightened his back against the truck's canvas wall and held his peace.

***

Stiles squinted at the map and peered out into the gloom.

'I reckon we should be getting close,' he said.

'There,' Mumford said. 'A soldier by the side of the road.'

The Frenchman's blue uniform lent him a spectral air in the first filtering of pre-dawn light. His face glowed like burnished leather as he sucked the last smoke from the cigarette held between his lips. Mumford pulled up next to the man and let his window down. The soldier spat his cigarette butt into the mud and scanned the typed order that Mumford held out. The man nodded and pointed up a track that edged the field behind him.

Mumford hauled the steering wheel over and drove carefully off the road. The track led them across the field and through a band of stunted trees. On the other side of the woodland strip, there were several French army trucks parked up. Another blue-clad soldier indicated they should park next to them.

Mumford shut down the engine, and he and Stiles clambered out. Stiles approached the soldier while Mumford unhitched the tailgate for the others to disembark.

The Frenchman looked at the British officer's cap badge and pointed further along the track.

'Là-bas' – his moist eyes avoided contact – 's'il vous plaît, Capitaine.'

Stiles and his companions followed the directions and walked past the French trucks. From one of them the tense voices of several men leaked into the chill air.

The party walked up the track until it veered left into what they recognised as an empty ammo dump. Roughly square, it had been dug several feet deep with the spoil heaped around the edges. A gap in this embankment allowed access down a shallow, hard-packed ramp. Along one side of the enclosure, a contingent of approximately fifty French soldiers stood, many with heads bowed. A few yards in front of these men, a dozen rifles lay evenly spaced on the ground.

A French officer stepped forward and pointed to the far corner beyond the assembled Frenchmen. Stiles led his group along the front of the soldiers, between them and the rifles. They reached the end of the crowd and formed a ragged line in the small space that had been left for them.

Across the other side of the pit, the earth wall had been neatly lined with sandbags. A yard or so in front of that, two bark-stripped trunks stood upright in the ground, no more than seven-feet tall, straight, solid and impassive. Coils of rope lay on the ground close by each post. Away in the corner, two rough pine caskets leaned against the sandbags.

'Christ,' Stiles muttered under his breath.

The men stood in the cold air as the minutes ticked by. Swathes of condensing breath rose lazily above their heads and the chill of the hard earth penetrated their leather soles. Fingers of soft light filtered into the pit, lancing across the silent void and creeping slowly down the sandbagged wall to gleam like crowns on the greenwood tops of the execution stakes.

The throb and growl of an engine shattered the silence, growing louder as got closer. The truck pulled up by the entrance ramp and, with a final flourish of revs, clanked into stillness. Four French soldiers spilled from the tailgate and a fully robed priest climbed down from the cab. The soldiers leaned back across the open tailgate, reaching in to pull something off the truck while the priest walked a slow diagonal path across the enclosure to stand between the stakes. He turned to face the ranked witnesses and waited, his bible clutched to his abdomen.

The four soldiers walked down the ramp, each pair staggering slightly with the awkward weight of their living burden. The two condemned men were trussed from shoulder to ankle with several coils of rope, rendering them unable to move at all. Their heads were thickly wrapped in bandages which hid their faces, but left a gap at their nostrils through which their ragged breathing rasped. A square of yellow fabric was pinned over their hearts, incongruously clean and bright against the dirt-grimed blue of their tunics.

When they reached the stakes, the soldiers shimmied around to plant the foot-end of their trussed burden on the ground against the wood, then pushed their parcel upright. One carrier leaned against the swaddled body, holding it in place while his fellow stooped to retrieve the ropes from the ground. The men worked swiftly to tie the bodies at shoulder, waist and ankle, then retreated to stand in the corner by the coffins.

The priest moved to the first prisoner. Leaning close to his head, he mumbled a few words and crossed himself. He repeated this with the second man, then walked back across the enclosure, up the ramp and out of sight.

A squad of six French soldiers marched down the ramp, picked up a rifle each and stood to attention facing the crowd of witnesses, their backs resolutely turned on the condemned men tied to the stakes. A second squad of six marched in, retrieved the remaining weapons and adopted the same stance. Their officer followed them and stood at the end of their line. The officer looked around the execution pit to check all was ready. Satisfied, he held a hand aloft, cast a look down the line of the firing squad, then dropped his hand back to his side.

The twelve soldiers swivelled on their heels, raised their weapons and took aim. The officer barked a single word and the dawn's quiet was torn apart by the ragged clatter of rifle fire.

The squad immediately turned their backs on their deed and returned to attention, facing the witnesses. Another shouted order rang out and the twelve riflemen turned right and marched quickly out of the pit. The officer walked over to the stakes, pulling his pistol from its holster as he went.

Both bodies had slumped as far as their bonds allowed. The punctured squares of yellow fabric seeped black with the sluggish ooze of blood from clustered wounds. Dust, expelled from the dirt-grimed tunics by the bullet impacts, hung suspended in the dawn light like the ethereal manifestation of liberated souls.

The officer held his ear close to the face of each body for several moments. Satisfied there was no need for further intervention, he holstered his pistol and shouted more orders. The French witnesses turned as one and shuffled towards the ramp. The officer watched them with a critical eye for a moment, then walked across to where Stiles and his men stood in quiet isolation.

'Merci, Capitaine.' The Frenchman pulled off his glove and extended his hand.

Stiles looked at the hand and then back into the man's eyes.

'Fuck off,' he said quietly.

The officer smiled, clicked his heels, and walked briskly away after his soldiers. Stiles looked back to the crumpled bodies sagging from the splintered posts. The four attendants had moved the caskets closer and were busy untying the cadavers.

'Come on chaps,' he said to his companions. 'Let's go home.'

He looked into the faces of his men as they passed him. All were tight with strain and pale from shock, but Benn's moist eyes flashed with a mixture of fear and outrage. Stiles followed them out of the pit. They skirted the mass of French soldiers climbing onto trucks and found their own vehicle. Stiles caught Mumford by the arm.

'I'll travel in the back with the others,' he muttered under his breath. 'They might need some steadying.'

Mumford nodded and climbed into the cab. Stiles swung into the back behind the other pilots and pulled up the tailgate. The four men sat down as the engine rumbled into life and the gears clashed into reverse, Stiles and Benn on one side, Minton and Morris on the other. The truck whined backwards through a quarter-circle. The gears ground again and the vehicle lurched away down the track towards the road.

'Well done chaps,' Stiles said. 'That was a bit grimmer than I'd expected.'

Benn let out a gasp, somewhere between a cough and a sob, like he'd been holding his breath against a foul stench.

'The priest just left them to it.' His voice was stretched across his distress. 'The priest walked away and abandoned them. He left them to die alone.'

'I don't know if that's fair…' Stiles began.

'Would it help' – Morris interrupted the captain – 'if *I* said some words for them?'

'Yes' – Benn nodded with a short, quick movement – 'it would.'

Morris pulled the book of psalms from inside his greatcoat and flipped through the pages. Finding his place, he held the book up, straightened his shoulders and began to read out loud.

'Thou carriest the children of men away as with a flood. They are as asleep. In the morning they are like the grass which groweth up. In the morning it flourisheth and groweth up In the evening it is cut down and withereth. For we are consumed by Thine anger, and by Thy wrath are we troubled.'

Benn subsided into himself, closed his eyes and leaned his head against his captain's shoulder.

***

Candles flickered on the farmhouse table. Dinner had been eaten and a melancholic torpidity hung over the heads of the assembled officers. Claypole stood, walked to the kitchen cabinet and retrieved a bottle of whisky and four small glasses. He returned to the table and poured out four measures. He pushed one across to Hartley, one to Stiles and then stopped, suddenly flummoxed with the realisation that he'd poured a drink for Davenport.

'I'll take it,' Mumford said.

'I thought you didn't drink,' Claypole said.

'I don't normally' – Mumford reached for the glass – 'but today's been a bit different.'

Claypole's gaze darted across to Stiles.

'How was it, Harry? Today?' he asked.

Stiles took a sip of his whisky.

'It was all quite efficient, from a military perspective I suppose,' Stiles said.

'But?' Claypole interjected.

'But... I don't believe that's any way to treat your fellow man,' Stiles finished.

'It was a punishment for their crime,' Hartley said. 'We all know the rules.'

'They were treated worse than rabid dogs,' Stiles said, his voice hardening slightly. 'There are more appropriate punishments than cold-blooded murder.'

Claypole held up his hand to forestall Hartley's nascent reply, then turned his attention back to Stiles.

'The French had a problem, and they found a solution,' he said. 'Jackdaw Squadron has a problem also, and it follows that we also need to find a solution.'

Stiles remained silent.

'Morris,' Claypole pressed the point. 'What's happening about Second Lieutenant Morris?'

Stiles drained his glass, swilling the spirit around his teeth before swallowing.

'He's fundamentally a good man,' he said. 'He's steady in his faith. He always follows orders-'

'Then order him to *shoot* at something.' Claypole thumped the table in emphasis. 'No more excuses.'

'Yes, sir,' Stiles said quietly. 'No more excuses.'

Chapter 18

Sunday, 15 April 1917

Claypole cocked his head at the sound of the dispatch rider and went to the door to accept the message tube. He dropped the messages on the table and ambled to the stove to pour a coffee. Mumford shuffled past him in full flying kit.

'Are you taking over from Harry?' Claypole asked.

'Yes, he should be back any time now.'

Mumford left and Claypole took his coffee to the table. He sat down and leafed through the dispatches. Hartley sat in one of the armchairs, smearing dubbin on a boot.

'Any news worth hearing,' he asked.

'Yes,' Claypole answered. 'We're getting twelve replacements. They'll be flying in tomorrow.'

'Good show,' Hartley said.

Claypole picked up a different slip of paper and scanned the typed message.

'Ah' – he smiled to himself – 'some more good news.'

The distant rattle of returning Pups snagged at his attention. He stood up and retrieved his greatcoat from its peg. Wrapping his muffler around his neck he left the farmhouse, crossed the road and walked briskly across the field. Overhead, three biplanes lined up to land.

'Damn it,' Claypole hissed to himself: Four scouts had set off an hour or so earlier.

He squinted against the hazy sunlight at the approaching aircraft, releasing a sigh of relief when he recognised the leading plane held Captain Stiles.

Stiles dropped in for a deft landing and taxied away to one side, clearing the way for the others. Claypole loped up his aircraft as the propellor clanked to a standstill.

'What happened, Harry?' Claypole shouted up to the cockpit.

Startled, Stiles squirmed around in his seat. Lifting his goggles to his forehead he spoke through his Vaseline smeared mask of silk.

'We got jumped, sir,' he said. 'Four, maybe five of them. One of them was that bloody red bastard. We had a hell of a scrap. We lost Platt. Two of them latched onto him like ticks.'

'Damn it to hell!' Claypole shouted.

Claypole stalked to the next aircraft as it came to rest. It was Potter's weary face that turned to peer at him from the cockpit. Claypole turned as the last biplane touched down. He ran out onto the field waving his arms. The aircraft slowed to a standstill as Claypole reached it and jumped onto the wing root.

'Keep the engine running, sonny,' Claypole shouted into Morris's shocked visage.

Claypole reached forward and groped around the breech-block. The loaded ammunition belt fed in on the left-hand side, but no empty belt fed out the other side. Claypole rounded Morris.

'Fly the bloody patrol again!' Claypole shouted.

'I beg your pardon?' Morris stammered.

'You heard me.' Spittle foamed into the corners of Claypole's mouth. 'Fly the patrol again. You *will* take part in this war if it's the last fucking thing you do!'

Claypole jumped off the wing and stalked away towards the other two planes. Behind him, Morris revved the engine and started his take-off run.

Stiles and Potter had climbed out of their scouts and they stood together watching. Claypole reached them, his immediate flush of anger beginning to subside.

'What's happening?' Stiles asked.

'He's flying the patrol again.' Claypole's voice glittered like hardened steel.

'On his own?' Stiles was incredulous. 'That's madness.'

'It'll bump him into reconsidering his attitude,' Claypole said. 'He's thinking about it right now, mark my words. When he realises he has no choice but to fight *with* us, he'll turn around and come back. He'll see sense.'

Stiles squinted up at the receding Pup.

'What if he obeys your order and flies the whole patrol?' he asked.

Mumford joined the small group.

'Am I alright to take my patrol up now?' he asked.

'No,' Claypole snapped. 'No-one flies from this field until Morris gets back.' He turned to Stiles. 'As soon as he's back, bring him to me.'

Claypole stalked away towards the farmhouse.

***

Stiles stood and waited as the time dragged past him. He pulled his flying helmet from his head and peeled his stocking mask off his face. He regarded the greasy tube of silk hanging limp in his hand for a moment, then dropped it to the ground, as if suddenly aware of its absurdity. He screwed his leather helmet back onto his crown and returned his gaze to the eastern horizon. The watery sunlight nudged his shadow across the grass, stretching it as it moved, playing the solitary man for a sundial, counting out the remainder of the day. The solid chill of clay seeped from the damp earth through the soles of his boots, numbing his toes and burning his heels. He ignored the furtive stares from the troubled faces that appeared every now and then at the mess windows. The occasional shout and the clatter of a dropped tool drifting from the hangar did not penetrate his consciousness. The Vaseline on his cheeks dried to crumbling flakes that curled away from his skin. The afternoon began its slow surrender to the insidious tendrils of the invading dusk, and the sky remained empty.

The brittle crash of breaking glass twisted Harry's head towards the pilots' mess. A wooden chair protruded through a smashed window and shouts spilled out into the evening air.

Stiles jogged across to the building and opened the door.

Benn was stamping around the room, kicking over tables and toppling chairs, his face contorted by his fury.

Stiles stepped inside and closed the door to contain the commotion. Potter and Clamp stood by the door.

'He's lost his reason, sir,' Potter hissed. 'He's trying to get out so he can go to the farmhouse. He saw what the major did with Morris. It's pushed him off his trolley.'

'The callous, murdering bastard,' Benn howled into the rafters. 'Let me get my hands on him!'

Stiles stepped forward into the room, leaving Potter and Clamp to block off the exit.

'Lieutenant Benn!' Harry's voice was firm but steady.

Benn subsided and turned slowly to face the captain.

'You're a decent man,' Benn implored. 'You've seen what he does. You saw what he just did to Morris. We need to get rid of-'

'Be quiet now!' Stiles interrupted him. 'We might be able to mend this as it stands. But you need to shut up.'

Benn's head drooped as he absorbed the moment. Over Benn's shoulder Stiles glimpsed Minton emerging from the dormitories. The big man padded forward on stockinged feet and he held a blanket up in front of him, poised as if to catch an unwary bird.

Benn raised his head and Stiles immediately caught his eye and held a finger to his own lips.

'I will deal with what's happened about Morris,' Stiles said quietly. 'He is a part of my flight. I'll be the one to ask any questions.'

Benn opened his mouth to answer, but his words were truncated by the blanket that dropped over his head. Minton bear-hugged Benn's arms to his side and Potter advanced, pulling off his belt to secure the man's flailing legs.

Stiles turned to Clamp: 'Go and fetch the medical officer,' he said. 'Tell him I want Benn hospitalised. I want him off this field as soon as possible. And get a carpenter to board up the window.'

He turned back to where Benn lay on the floor. The man had surrendered to his restraint and had collapsed into blanket-muffled sobbing.

A sudden anger flared in Harry's chest and he spun on his heel and left the mess. He strode across the field, over the muddied road and up the farmhouse steps. He paused and breathed deeply, forcing himself down from his anger's apex, bargaining his emotion away against the obligations of rank. He opened the door and stepped into the farmhouse.

Claypole sat at the table with his hands folded in his lap, a single sheet of paper lay before him. His brows cast dark shadows across his eyes, emphasising the bones in his cheeks and the unhealthy pallor of his skin where the day's stubble gleamed prematurely grey.

'Morris didn't come back,' Stiles said, holding his voice level. 'Your order has led directly to his unnecessary death.'

'What did you think of Lieutenant Platt, Harry?' Claypole leaned back in his chair, the shadows vanished from his face and his eyes flashed with challenge.

'What do you mean?' Stiles spluttered.

'When you got back from patrol you told me you'd *lost* Platt, like he was a glove or a handkerchief. Now that we've *lost* Morris, you seem to think it's important enough to accuse your commanding officer of' – Claypole cast around for the word – 'misconduct.'

'Morris is dead because of something *you* chose to do,' Stiles said. 'I don't know if misconduct even starts to cover it.'

Claypole surged to his feet sending his chair clattering to the floor.

'Platt died because of something Morris chose *not* to do. There were three guns on that patrol when there should have been four.' Claypole's voice stretched with suppressed anger. 'It's not a fucking flying club, Harry. We're here to kill Germans. That is our *only* purpose. Because if we don't kill enough of them, they're going to win this bloody war, and if that happens, what price Morris' confession boxes in pretty little English churches when they're all owned and run by the bloody Kaiser?'

Stiles dropped his chin to his chest, his outrage punctured.

'What a bloody shambles,' he said quietly. 'How do I explain this to the men? How do I defend what we're doing to each other?'

'You don't have to, Harry.' Claypole's voice dropped to its normal tone. He picked up the slip of paper from the table. 'Your leave has been reinstated. Two weeks. I've organised your transport for the morning.'

Monday, 16 April 1917

Stiles stood at the farmhouse window gazing at the twelve new Sopwith Pups standing in two lines of six along the edges of Vert Galant field, their freshly doped wings reflecting the reluctant sunlight. At least the new boys were good at parking, he mused to himself.

'Captain Mumford,' Claypole called. 'Get the replacements over here, please. I think I might like to introduce myself.'

Mumford pushed through the door and Stiles watched him wend across the field towards the mess.

'Is there anything you want me to do when I'm in England?' Stiles asked without turning from the window. 'Anyone you'd like me to visit for you?'

'You might drop in on Davenport, if you can?' Claypole said. 'He was assigned a bed in the Royal Victoria Patriotic. It might cheer him up to see a familiar face.'

A gaggle of men spilled out of the mess and walked towards the farmhouse, Mumford at their head. Stiles crossed to the coat stand and pulled on his greatcoat.

'Yes, it might,' he said. 'I'll drop by, see if he's still there.'

Mumford stuck his head around the door.

'The new intake is ready for you, Major,' he said and ducked outside again.

Claypole went to retrieve his own coat. He shrugged it onto his shoulders and extended his hand to Stiles.

'Whatever else happens, Harry, I look upon you as a friend,' he said. 'If we both get through this war, I hope *that* will survive as well.'

Stiles accepted the handshake.

'I'm sure it will, sir,' he said.

Claypole opened the door and went outside. Stiles picked up his battered leather suitcase and followed him.

The new pilots were lined up in two rows of six in front of the farmhouse. Stiles drifted off to one side, eyeing the road for signs of his transport. Claypole descended the steps to stand in front of the serried men.

'Gentlemen,' he said, 'I'm sure you've read the newspaper reports about what was going on in this sector only one week ago. The capture of Vimy Ridge was a famous victory indeed, but it was not a decisive victory. Perforce, the war grinds on.' He paused, cocked his head and pointed vaguely at the southern sky: 'That noise you can hear is the support barrage for a major French offensive which began this morning. I believe, certainly in staff circles, a major breakthrough is the expected result.

'In any event, I am Major Claypole, commander of Jackdaw Squadron.' He began pacing along the line of men. 'Our current task is to occupy the German forces in front of us to prevent them moving south to interfere with the French assault. As you are new to this game, I'm going to give you all a few bits of hard-won RFC wisdom.

'Keep in formation for as long as you can. Lone wolves will very soon be…' He paused in his pacing, stopped by his own words. 'Flying alone' – he rephrased – 'will only invite trouble.' He resumed his slow walk down the line.

'Avoid diving away from an enemy. The Pup is generally superior in the climb. Do not engage a superior force if it can be avoided, although this little nugget may find itself overruled by a general order if things are especially hairy on the ground. Make sure you always look above and behind…'

Claypole's ongoing lecture was lost to Stiles as his transport clattered to a halt on the road next to him. Stiles placed his suitcase into the back of the truck and climbed into the cab. The driver nodded in salute and pulled away.

Something knitted Harry's brow with trouble. He had listened to Claypole's welcome speech at least half-a-dozen times; this time something was different...

'He didn't ask their names,' he spoke the thought out loud.

'I'm sorry, sir,' the driver said.

'Nothing,' Stiles said. 'It's not important.'

Chapter 19

Monday, 23 April 1917 – South London

The doorbell chimed and Harry listened to his wife's footsteps clacking on the tiled hallway. She opened the door and a draught of chilled air swirled into the drawing room where he sat. The front door closed and his wife came into the room with a bulky package wrapped in brown paper.

'Your uniforms, back from the cleaners.' She placed the package on the table. 'Do you have plans for today?'

'Yes, I do,' Harry said. 'I'm off to the Royal Victoria. One of the officers from Jackdaw Squadron knocked himself about a bit and they sent him there to get patched up.' He stood up and retrieved his jacket from a chair. 'I've been putting it off, but I really must just bite the bullet.'

'Then let me press a uniform for you,' his wife said. 'Can't have you going to a military hospital in your weekend tweeds.'

'Please don't bother, my love,' Harry said, walking through to the coatrack in the hallway. 'I'm not in any hurry to put that back on. My tweeds are fine.'

'Well' – she bustled past him towards the kitchen – 'there *is* one thing you need.'

Harry pulled on his overcoat and settled his hat on his head.

'A buttonhole!' Harry's wife returned and pinned the tight bud of a deep red rose to the lapel of his overcoat. 'That finishes you off nicely.'

'Thank you, my love.' Harry bent to kiss her lips. 'I shan't be long.'

***

The Royal Victoria Patriotic Building sat square and solemn, its yellow brick façade somewhat softening the severity of its neo-gothic gravitas. Along the edges of its driveway, its manicured flower-beds finally unfurled leaf and bud to greet the retarded spring. At the centre of the edifice, a squat tower overbore the doors, flanked by window-lined wings that terminated in lesser towers. The steep-pitched roof of each tower bore spires and turrets, lending an air of French chateau to the building's prosaic municipal genesis.

Harry walked through the entrance and approached the nurse at the reception desk. She raised her head from her paperwork as he approached and smiled her silent question.

'I've come to visit Captain Davenport, RFC.' Harry's hushed tone reverberated around the large stone hallway. 'Back injury, as I understand it.'

'And you are?' Her smile remained fixed.

'Captain Stiles, from his squadron.' He plucked apologetically at the cloth of his overcoat: 'I'm on leave.'

Her smile warmed a degree: 'Follow me, sir.'

Harry trailed behind the nurse down a door-lined corridor that terminated in French doors leading onto an enclosed courtyard. She opened the door and stood back.

'The captain is over there' – she pointed – 'in the corner.'

Harry nodded his thanks and stepped through the door onto the flagstones beyond.

Davenport sat in a bath-chair with his legs and torso swathed in grey blankets. A dark scab straddled the bridge of his nose and his eye sockets held the shadows of bruising. A young man wearing infantry uniform sat on a wooden bench next to him, a crutch leaned by his side. Davenport noticed the other man approaching.

'Goodness,' he said. 'Harry! How the devil are you?'

'I'm well enough.' Harry extended his hand and Davenport clasped it tight.

'Forgive me if I don't stand, old man,' he said. 'The pins don't work anymore.'

Harry turned to the young man who had hauled himself upright, propped that way by the crutch under his right arm. Harry noticed the lad's right leg was missing below the knee and his trouser leg was neatly folded up and pinned on the outside.

'Forgive me,' Davenport blustered. 'This is Charlie. Charlie, this is Captain Stiles. He flies with Jackdaw Squadron' – his tone fluttered slightly – 'my old squadron.'

'It's an honour to meet you, sir,' Charlie said. 'I'll leave you to visit in peace.'

Davenport watched Charlie's back as he halted his way towards the French doors.

'He's been a real boon,' Davenport said. 'He says it was his dream to become a pilot. When he spotted my cap badge, he was cheeky enough to

165

waylay me with his questions. He quite made me forget the mess I'm in. He's such an… infectious joy.'

Charlie disappeared through the doors and Davenport shifted his gaze to Harry's face.

'He was wounded on Vimy Ridge, the day before I pulled off my monumental landing cock-up. We were admitted here on the same day, so it's quite likely we were on the same hospital ship across the channel.'

Harry lowered himself onto the bench and removed his hat.

'They did their best to save Charlie's leg,' Davenport continued. 'But the gangrene got into him.' He threw a clenched look of contempt at the impassive sandstone walls: 'The wards here reek of gangrene. The stench clings in your nostrils and settles into the pit of your stomach.'

He fell silent for a moment, his gaze flicking across the yellow bricks. When his eyes rested again on Harry's face, they glistened with emotion.

'I was glad when they cut off his leg,' his lips pursed against the upswell in his chest. 'I was glad, even though it dashed his dreams of flying. I was glad because it meant he wouldn't have to go back to France. And the price he's had to pay to escape that hell' – he slapped a hand onto his blanket-wrapped, unfeeling leg – 'isn't, on balance, so very great.'

***

The sun cracked its way through the clouds as Stiles left the hospital. He let the rays bathe his upturned face and diverted his way onto Wandsworth Common for a stroll.

The paths were not crowded; here and there a pair of women or a uniformed man and his sweetheart drifted through the warming air.

Harry noted a single woman coming towards him. Her well-fitted dress was of a vibrant red silk and she wore a wide-brimmed hat of black velvet with a spray of ostrich feathers.

Stiles moved to the side of the path as she approached, but the woman stepped across to match him. Confused, Harry stopped as the woman walked up to him, staring with challenge into his eyes.

'It's lovely and peaceful, isn't it?' she said. 'Such a lovely day for a promenade in the sun.'

'Why, yes' – Harry tipped his hat – 'now that spring is here.'

'But I have to ask' – her eyes narrowed – 'what are *you* doing here, when you should be in France with our heroes?'

She plucked Harry's rose from his lapel with black-gloved fingers and threw it to the ground. She then deftly plucked a white feather from her hat and pushed it into his buttonhole.

Harry looked at the rose on the ground, the white feather on his coat and back into the woman's eyes.

'How is it that you can tell the difference between cowards and heroes?' he asked quietly. 'You? With your maid to tie your corset, draw your bath and pour your afternoon tea, how do you know the difference?' He pulled the feather from his buttonhole and held it in front of the woman's nose like a dagger. 'I've been at the frontline for over a year now, and I still can't tell the difference.'

The woman's face stayed still, only a slight flush beneath her eyes betrayed her. She raised her hand and took hold of the feather.

'Excuse me' – Harry brushed a few stray white strands from his coat – 'I've taken up too much of your time.'

Postscript

Tuesday, 1 May 1917 – RFC Headquarters, France

Lieutenant Colonel Tarquin Beadle sat at his desk listening to the log fire crackling in the grate. His eyes fell on his desk calendar. He reached across and tore the last day of April from its face, screwed the square of paper into a ball and flicked it across the room into the flames.

There was a brief knock at the door and a staff officer entered carrying a slim file.

'The numbers have come through, sir,' he said.

'Ah, good.' Beadle rubbed his hands together. 'What does the balance sheet look like?'

'In the month of April, we lost' – the other man flipped open the file and ran his finger down the listing inside – '245 aircraft together with 400 aircrew, more than half of those were killed.'

Beadle pursed his lips: 'And our score was?'

'Our best estimate is that we lost at least three times more than the enemy,' the staff officer said. 'It's all in here.' He laid the folder on the desk. 'Is there anything else, sir.'

'Yes.' Beadle returned his gaze to the fire. 'Find out what's for lunch, will you?'

I hope you have enjoyed Farewell to the Glory Boys and will consider leaving an honest review on Amazon.

Visit my website at www.melvynfickling.com and sign up for the Bluebirds Newsletter for updates on my forthcoming work.

Please consider liking my page at Facebook.com/MelvynFicklingAuthor

Author's notes

This is a historical novel based on real events. It is not a history of those events or of the people who found themselves entangled in those events.

All characters are entirely fictional. Any similarity these characters may bear to persons living or dead is coincidental.

Locations are real, although the details of real locations have been fictionalised in a sympathetic manner.

The backdrop of events against which the novel is set is well documented elsewhere. I have kept as close as possible to the actual timeline, but some events may have been shifted slightly to accommodate plot requirements. No disrespect is implied or intended to the people who were involved in those events.

Sources

Fighters 1914-19 – Kenneth Munson

Aircraft of World War I – Jack Herris and Bob Pearson

Fighter Heroes of WWI – Joshua Levine

Bloody April – Peter Hart

Cheerful Sacrifice – Jonathan Nicholls

A Taste of Success – Jim Smithson

Vimy Ridge – Alexander McKee

Fighting in the Air 1916 to 1945 – RAF Museum Series Volume 7

Made in the USA
Las Vegas, NV
11 January 2024